I0671908

Midsummer Nights

Newly arrived at Oberon's court, Puck has already made a name for himself through his wit, his wiliness, and his very nice legs. But he's not interested in the envy of his peers; what he's really after is the attention of the lord of all fairies himself. Seducing the monarch will surely win him power and prestige, provided he can withstand Oberon's famously bad temper.

Soon, though, Puck realizes that Oberon's belligerent façade is just that, and his schemes of strategic seduction are submerged beneath budding infatuation. Now, Puck will have to muster all his tricks, from sonnets to the lash, to win the fairy king's heart—a task which becomes substantially more difficult when Oberon discovers that Puck has been consorting with mortals...

Midsummer Sky

No one knows why Oberon, king of the greatest fairy court in the world, doesn't have wings. Not even his crafty lover, Puck, who prides himself on being privy to all Oberon's secrets. But that's about to change, for Oberon's mother has revealed to her son that there may be a way to regain his lost wings—provided Oberon is willing to risk losing Puck...

Midsummer Court

While Titania is visiting her relatives, Oberon is left to govern the fairy court in her absence, with Puck, his lover and adviser, at his side. Despite Puck's efforts to drag the king away from his duties and towards more salacious pursuits, Oberon remains loved and respected by the majority of his people. But trouble looms on the horizon; Oberon's rumoured perversity and failure to produce an heir have earned him a handful of political enemies. When disaster strikes the court at the solstice feast, they are quick to point the finger of blame at the one they hold responsible for Oberon's weaknesses—Puck himself.

This is a work of fiction. All characters, places and events are from the author's imagination and should not be confused with fact. Any resemblance to persons, living or dead, events or places is purely coincidental.

Copyright 2016 by T.J. Land

All rights reserved, including the right of reproduction in whole or in part in any form.

Published by
NineStar Press
PO Box 91792
Albuquerque, New Mexico, 87199
www.ninestarpress.com

Warning: This book contains sexually explicit content which is only suitable for mature readers.

Print ISBN #978-1-945952-11-1
Cover by Natasha Snow
Edited by Raevyn

No part of this publication may be reproduced in any material form, whether by printing, photocopying, scanning or otherwise without the written permission of the publisher, NineStar Press, LLC

Bad Fairies

The Collection

T.J. Land

Dedication

To William, with my love and apologies.

Midsummer Nights

Chapter One

Word spread quickly through the court; Oberon's new servant was going to be a problem.

Foremost in the compilation of evidence were his legs. They made up two thirds of his height and were rarely covered in much more than a butterfly-wing skirt that barely afforded him decency and dozens of tattoos that made it seem as though his skin was sprouting leaves.

Ignoring them was a fool's errand. When the new servant walked, he strutted, and when at rest, he would lean against walls, furniture, and often Oberon himself, his gorgeous legs stretched out for all to see.

"Shameless," tutted Titania's maids, each one of whom would have happily murdered her sisters for a chance to trace one of the painted leaves with her fingertips.

What made it worse was that he was clearly a foreigner, with his peculiar accent and curly black hair. No one could work out where Oberon had found him, although rumours abounded. Some said he had come from the moon. Others said he was actually the child of a demigod, abandoned among mortals until Oberon had espied him and stolen him away. And even others said he was a lump of clay into which Oberon, for his own personal amusement, had breathed life.

Nevertheless, whatever their opinions on his origins, all agreed it was in no way proper.

"King Oberon has not walked below my branches for days," sighed the willow.

"His Majesty lavishes all his attention on the newcomer," muttered the river sprites bitterly.

"Our sweet and fearsome king has not asked us to sing for him in weeks," wept the swallows, and in their sorrow, they departed for warmer climes; though it was a most unseasonal time to do so.

Titania, for her part, was delighted.

It was no secret that theirs was an unhappy marriage, and her husband's new toy had a knack for keeping them out of one another's hair. What was more, he was unfailingly polite, and his presence seemed to boost her handmaidens' morale.

"You could go far, Puck," she told him, seated on her throne of peacock feathers.

He bowed. "Thank you, Your Majesty."

"My only concern is whether or not you will be able to cope with my husband's temperament in the long run. He can be...difficult."

With wide eyes, black and bright as two beetles, Puck said, "I am honoured to serve my king and my queen in whatever capacity they ask of me."

Titania, who was no fool, merely smirked and sent him on his way.

☆☆☆

Puck found Oberon standing alone in the grove where the hedgehog mushrooms grew, his arms clasped behind his back. He was brooding.

This was not an uncommon state of affairs. Despite the fiery façade his liege presented to the world, Puck had come to realize that Oberon was, by nature, deeply melancholic.

"Majesty," he said, bowing as he approached.

Oberon growled, the noise deep and not unlike that of an ancient crocodile Puck had once known. As a greeting, it was less hostile than habitual; his liege was not given to pleasantries.

"What do you want, sprite?"

A quick flutter of his wings took Puck to Oberon's side, where he stood in the shade of a large toadstool. He was considerably shorter than the fairy king, who, at eight inches, towered over most of his court; the top of his pointed ears were barely level with Oberon's breastbone. "Merely to greet my gracious lord and inquire as to whether I might be of service to him this day?"

He laced his tone with enough insinuation as to make his meaning clear. He had now been in service to Oberon for half a summer, but despite performing—if he did say so himself—magnificently and proving himself the equal of any task Oberon could throw at him, his master had not yet made use of his body.

Puck wasn't quite sure why.

That the king had no taste for women was an open secret. That Puck was exactly to his taste seemed indicated by the number of times he had caught Oberon glancing at his legs. However, thus far there had been no solicitation, much less seduction. The two occasions on which Puck had attempted to flirt had gotten him nowhere at all.

It was all very frustrating. The prospect of weaselling his way into the bed of the most powerful fairy alive had been one of the main factors motivating his decision to surrender his wandering ways and settle at Oberon's court. He'd been confident of his ability to bend the king to his will within a week, but at this point, he was seriously beginning to suspect he had made a mistake.

When Oberon did not answer—but did not indicate his desire for Puck's departure by taking a swipe at him, as was his way—Puck bit his lip and peeked at his master's face. He only allowed himself two or three such peeks a day, fearing that overindulgence would immolate him or, at the very least, expose his intentions to all the world.

But ah, what a face it was. Strong jawed, sharp eyed, lean and cold and cruel, like a wolf in winter. Oberon wore no beard—and indeed, what an injustice it would be to conceal a chin like that—but his silver-grey hair grew down to his shoulders, thick and mane-like, and Puck had often dreamed of burying his face in it. Alas, Oberon had no wings—speculation as to what had happened to them was rife among gossipy sprites—but his broad, tapering back more than made up for it.

"Titania inquires after your welfare, master," Puck said to fill the silence (and to disrupt the flow of his own thoughts, which, thanks to the nearness of Oberon's scent, were becoming progressively obscene).

"Did the queen send you in search of me?"

"She thinks she did. But sweet Puck would not have disturbed his master's peace upon her orders; sweet Puck was already in search of you, my liege."

And, as Puck knew well, he had only found him because Oberon had desired his presence. Had he truly wanted solitude, he would have turned himself into a tree, or a star, and Puck would have scoured the face of the earth in vain.

Tentatively, he added, "Has there been some quarrel, perhaps?"

It was, of course, a facetious question. The queen and the king quarrelled as often as they breathed.

"She desires my presence tonight. It is our anniversary," said Oberon, in black tones.

Ah.

Oberon and Titania's engagement had been a complicated business. The circumstances under which it had come to be were lost to the mists of time, and it was possible that, at one point, both of them had been quite happy with the prospect of an eternity in one another's company. Even so, it had always been a political marriage and, as such, had come with certain expectations and obligations placed on both parties. Fairies being fairies, the wedding ceremony had included a recitation of vows enforced by ancient, powerful incantations, the breaking of which would activate a host of particularly nasty curses. The upshot was that, until such time as an heir was provided, husband and wife were bound by magical law to make, at the very least, one attempt each year to produce one.

By mutual agreement, this attempt took place on their anniversary. By all accounts, in nearly one thousand years, it had not once resulted in anything more than two utterly filthy regal moods that lasted for weeks on end.

"Perhaps she will have a gift for you," Puck said. "Or perhaps you would like me to find a gift for you to give to her? I have some ideas..."

"We do not exchange gifts."

"Oh. Well, maybe a nice meal, or some charming musical entertainment to commemorate the occasion..."

Oberon glared at him balefully.

"...or not."

Puck racked his brains. He snapped his fingers. "My liege, consider this; what if I were to go deep into the woods, procure a squirrel or weasel, and devise some spell to transform it into a fairy child? I am a skilled craftsman; no one would ever know. You could show it to the world and..."

A strange sound echoed off the boughs of the willow trees that stood as sentinels around the grove, setting birds to flight. Oberon was laughing.

"I do not jest, my liege," said Puck, a touch hurt, as Oberon bent over double, his massive shoulders shaking. "Do you doubt my skill? Or my capacity for keeping secrets? I assure you, I..."

"No, no," Oberon said as he recovered, shaking his head. "No, you...you misunderstand. I do not doubt you in the least, sprite. But your plan—amusing as it is—will not work. The enchanted vows I took will not be fooled by such tricks."

He snorted again, muffling the sound behind a palm. "In truth, I thought you were going to offer to devise some potion that would enable me to take some degree of pleasure in the act. That is what previous servants have done."

"Is that what my liege asks of me?"

"No. I have no desire to change my nature, even temporarily. Besides, I have come to believe that Titania has no desire to be a mother at all. At least, not to any spawn of mine."

"A sensible queen," said Puck, nodding in approval. "Children are horrid."

One of Oberon's mighty eyebrows twitched upward at that, and

Puck was worried he had overstepped (and worried also that he had now spent altogether too long staring at the king's face). But amusement still played at the corners of Oberon's mouth, and he said, "Regardless of their merits, I am obliged to engender one, and to do so in the traditional manner. The only way out would be for Titania or myself to dissolve the marriage, and neither of us is willing to do so."

"But why not, master? If it brings you such displeasure?"

"Because, nosy one, I enjoy being king ever so slightly more than I would enjoy not being my wife's husband."

Puck could see the logic in this. Even so, he sighed.

For a while, they stood silently, Oberon's gaze fixed on the sky, Puck's on the surrounding fungus.

Slowly, Puck said, "Perhaps if my liege had something to look forward to afterwards...perhaps that would make the task itself less arduous?"

"What sort of thing would you suggest?" Oberon muttered, distracted by a passing flock of geese.

His wings twitching, Puck shifted his weight from one foot to the other. "Whatever would please my liege. A game...or some other gentle pastime..."

At last, Oberon's gaze snapped down to meet Puck's. His eyes were the colour of rubies, and a predatory intelligence lurked behind them.

"An apt proposal," he said at length. "Might you be able to devise such a game?"

It was the first time Oberon had asked him for something without ordering. Puck nodded, tilting his head in such a way as to allow a lock of his curly black hair to fall fetchingly across his cheek, hoping that the king might be inspired to lean in and brush it back.

Instead, Oberon resumed his original posture, returning his attention to the geese. "Very well."

Chapter Two

As per usual, fulfilling his marital obligations took Oberon a mortifying two hours, at the end of which he and Titania exchanged teeth-gritted pleasantries and fled one another's company as fast as they could.

He felt sullied and sullen and was about to indulge in a draught of blackberry wine when he remembered his new servant's suggestion. So foul was his mood that he almost dismissed the notion out of hand, but the memory of a sable lock lying across smooth skin pestered him. Eventually, grudgingly, Oberon took himself down to his private pond to wash off the smell of his failure, and then he headed for the grove.

Puck was waiting for him. He had, in fact, prepared a bed of chrysanthemum petals and feathers beneath a cluster of black trumpets. Deep inside, Oberon was faintly touched.

Even better, the sprite had the good sense not to ask him how it had gone. Instead, he executed a neat bow and said, "Well met, master."

"Well met," replied Oberon, with courtly politeness.

In truth, he wasn't entirely certain what to do next. Contrary to rumour, he'd had few affairs. His reputation for black humour and savagery in battle had preceded him, and previous would-be seducers had tried to attract his attention with gifts of swords, spears, and severed body parts, or else by challenging him to duels. That he might have more than one personality trait never seemed to occur to anyone. So, bored and frustrated, he usually lay alone.

Thankfully, after a moment's awkward silence, Puck tiptoed forward and, leaning up, offered Oberon his mouth. Oberon accepted it and found that Puck's lips were soft, and that his silvery tongue was hesitant.

Encouraged by the small sigh his ministrations provoked, Oberon plucked his servant from his feet and carried him over to the makeshift bed.

It quickly became apparent that Puck enjoyed being kissed, and having his wings stroked, and most of all, being enfolded in arms large enough to snap him in two. Oberon's previous partners had never asked tenderness of him—that wasn't why they had sought out a king to dally with—and he found himself repeatedly drawing back to check that he wasn't doing anything incorrectly.

Yet his size and solidity were plainly not unappreciated. Puck's nimble fingers kept pressing into his muscles, testing them as though they were ripening fruit, and every time Oberon flexed—himself not immune to the charms of exhibitionism—he would sigh, and sometimes shiver, and seek another kiss from his master's firm, cruel mouth.

"Sensualist," Oberon rumbled, meaning no real insult by it. He found his body reacting to Puck's worship far faster and with far more strength than he would have anticipated, and suspected a streak of hitherto unacknowledged sensuality in himself.

But soon, he detected something oddly stilted in his new lover's manner.

"What is it?" Oberon demanded, abandoning the slender neck onto which he had been biting a love-mark.

"Master," Puck said, in that high-pitched voice he used when he had been rehearsing something in his head, "while I am...er, grateful to be afforded the opportunity to share your body, I cannot help but feel...ah..."

"Yes?"

"Master, you are rather, er..."

"Spit it out."

"...big."

Oberon stared at him for a moment as he shifted in abashed

silence and then threw his head back and laughed madly.

"You thought I was going to ask you to take my cock?" he queried, quelling the cackles with effort.

"It would hardly be the first time you've set me to a nigh-impossible task," Puck replied indignantly.

Oberon slapped his arse, enjoying the way it made the smaller fairy shiver. "I would hardly expect this feeble thing to accommodate me, sprite. Your mouth, on the other hand, has always been the most disproportionate part of you."

Grinning, Puck replied, "Best to put it to good use then," and slithered down to Oberon's groin.

"Ah," Oberon sighed shakily; for in truth, he'd been contemplating Puck's mouth for almost as long as they'd known one another. "I thought you'd be good at this."

And indeed, Puck was as skilled in this as he was in all things, and he swallowed down Oberon's seed without a whimper of protest. More gratifying yet, when Oberon reached for Puck's cock to reward his efforts, he found that his new lover was already rock hard. He came within seconds, babbling inanities and shaking like a leaf.

"I've never done that before," Puck said moments later, slithering up to lie at Oberon's side.

Sprawled beside him with his chest steadily rising and falling and the back of his hand covering his eyes, Oberon made a noise of exasperation. "Will you never learn to hold your tongue, fool? You are now a member of a court of ruthless fae, all of whom look upon you with jealousy and mistrust. What would possess you to make such an admission? To me, of all people? Do you know nothing of my reputation?"

"Hardly an admission, my liege," Puck retorted, clearly indignant. (For Puck's part, he had to fight back the impulse to point out that, while Oberon clearly liked to think of himself as a Machiavellian tyrant, his reputation among his people was more to do with his good looks, sour temper, and famous kindness to all supplicants). "Your network of informants could have found out as much in half a day. In fact, in telling you myself before they could, I've probably just obtained a strategic advantage."

"Namely?"

"I've endeared myself to you."

"You think so?"

"Yes. It will flatter your pride to think of yourself as having stolen my innocence."

"Stop laughing," Puck said crossly a moment later.

With effort, Oberon gained control over himself. "My pride is sufficiently flattered by your earlier reference to my godhood."

Puck's jaw dropped in horror. "I didn't."

"As it happens, you did."

With a dismayed squeak, Puck buried his face in the petals. "Go away. Don't look at me. Don't talk to me. This is all your fault."

Rolling over, Oberon paused to admire the line of his back, the way his shoulders flared and tapered gracefully down to his narrow waist, and his petite rear. Reflecting upon the latter, he pinched it and said, "Tell me, sprite; do you always make that sound when someone spills their seed into your mouth, or did mine just taste particularly nice?"

"You are crude and deplorable," Puck mumbled, his hips shifting—pressing his (swelling, Oberon suspected) cock into the petals, while Oberon continued to fondle his arse idly.

"You certainly have a virgin's refractory period," Oberon observed, feeling heat begin to pool, yet again, in his groin.

Taking hold of Puck at the waist, he rolled him over and observed the flush running up his belly and across his chest, before leaning down. It had been some years since last he'd bestowed upon a lover the honour of his mouth. Even so, it was one of those things you never really forgot.

"Master," Puck panted as Oberon's hands cradled his narrow hips and lifted him off the bed.

He was smaller than Oberon was used to. Determining how best to pleasure him without hurting him—for he wasn't yet certain whether Puck enjoyed pain as much as he did, or in the same way—took the fairy lord a minute. He used his teeth only very carefully, grazing the underside of Puck's cock, and drew back slowly, until only the tip rested on his tongue. Nursing it for a moment—kissing it, really—he sank back down, noting the way Puck all but sobbed in need.

He had, Oberon admitted to himself, an ulterior motive for wanting to make an impression. Puck's own performance had easily been the best worshipping he had ever received, the sort of performance that could only be given by someone who truly, deeply loved having a cock down their throat. How he'd moaned around it, drool running from both corners of his mouth, silver tongue lapping...

Oberon became aware that his own hips had begun to rut against the petal bed and refocused his attention.

"You are suspiciously good at that," Puck told him. "Do you have concubines parading into your bedroom every night for you to practice on?"

"You have no other point of reference. I could be merely mediocre."

"You—ngh—don't do anything at which you are mediocre, master. If you aren't either good or excellent at something, you get someone else to do it. Ah!"

If he was telling the truth earlier, then this was the first time he'd had his cock in someone's mouth.

It was at that moment that Oberon privately resolved to ensure that the memory of said mouth would spoil Puck for all others. He redoubled his efforts, taking him as deep as he could, conscious that it wasn't nearly as deep as Puck had taken him. Still; quality over quantity, and all that.

Puck's long fingers sank into his hair, yanking hard enough to send a deeply satisfying wave of pain across his scalp. If his sprite hadn't yet been able to discern his proclivities, the way Oberon shuddered at that moment was probably enough to tip him off.

"Gods, but you're a hedonist," Puck said, thrusting sharply into his mouth. "Look at you. Whining for it."

His head fell back, and he keened as Oberon licked a stripe up his cock in retribution.

"Here's...here's a thought, my liege. I'll pull your hair some more, and you take yourself in hand. Now."

Yes, sir. The words appeared in Oberon's mind, so clear and uncontentious that he was horribly afraid he might have spoken them, had his mouth not been occupied. Almost without his telling it to do so, his hand slid around his cock.

"Good boy. Hmm. I wonder... Can you make yourself come before I do?"

Oberon had never been able to back down from a challenge, not once in his life. But there was something else at play in his renewed efforts to pleasure himself. It was strange and sweet to be commanded by his servant.

Puck's sharp fingernails raked across his scalp as Oberon swallowed his seed. Dizzy with pleasure, he wondered if they'd drawn blood and came into his fist with a shudder.

"Oh, master," sighed Puck, resuming his servile persona once again as he curled up against Oberon's chest.

Oberon grunted, wrapping an arm around his waist. "A good game, sprite."

"Well played, my liege."

Chapter Three

For all that he was old—older than rivers, older than mountains—and often melancholy, Oberon was a fairy king. As such, his rages were frequent and terrifying.

Puck hit the rock with enough force to break two of his ribs and one of his wings. He slid to the ground and lay whimpering in pain for a moment, before managing to get himself up onto his knees in a pose of supplication.

"My liege, please, forgive me. It was an honest mistake. An accident. If I..."

Oberon advanced on him, swift and terrible as a thundercloud, and struck his face with the back of his hand. Puck didn't try to dodge the blow; to do so would have been to invite two more.

"You have humiliated me," he hissed. "Humiliated me in front of my court, my wife, and the ambassadors. You miserable fool."

Puck's attempts to speak in his defence were thwarted as Oberon took hold of him by the neck and held him aloft. For a moment, he merely watched him squirm and choke with narrowed eyes, before throwing him into a nearby clump of stinging nettles.

"Remove yourself from my sight."

Puck wisely bit his tongue, and crawled away into the undergrowth.

☆☆☆

For the next few hours, Oberon paced back and forth before his throne, muttering to himself.

It was, upon reflection, at least partly his own fault.

Oberon had known the ambassadors from the elf tribes in the western marshlands would be volatile and prone to taking offence. It was to be expected; historically, they had received very poor treatment from the southern fairy courts. Oberon had spent much of his reign attempting to mend bridges his ancestors had cheerfully burned.

He had also known that their dietary preferences were highly specific: no meat, no fruit, no milk, only a limited number of vegetables, and *absolutely* no wine.

He had also known that Puck had bad blood with the ambassadors—an old friendship gone sour, by all accounts, although Oberon didn't know the specifics.

He had also known that Puck was in charge of the catering.

In the grand scheme of things, it wasn't a catastrophe. Oberon had managed to partially salvage the situation by publicly deriding his servant in the most abusive language possible, and the ambassadors had seemed somewhat mollified. But the event had endangered a week's worth of delicate negotiations, and worse, he had noticed Titania smirking at him from behind her fan.

Hellfire and damnation. He would need to make a formal apology. This, perhaps, was what infuriated him the most; for in truth, Oberon did not care for the elves and their superior ways any more than Puck did.

He stopped pacing and shook his head. There was no avoiding it. Titania would apologise on his behalf if he asked her, but he didn't care to put himself in his wife's debt.

Oberon donned his swallow-feather cape and went forth to make amends. The ambassadors had been honoured guests and, as such, given an entire tree to themselves in which to lodge. But though he scoured it from root to branch—feeling, as he climbed, the old pang of longing for his wings—he couldn't find either of them.

His heart sank. Had they taken such offence that they'd simply departed without a further word? No, no. Surely not. They were hostile, but not stupid. The trade agreements at stake would benefit their people just as much as his own. Most likely, they'd taken themselves to the river to swim or gone to visit the spectacular weavers' nest for which his court was renowned. He would return later.

Oberon's temper, by now, had cooled, and he recollected his earlier reprimand with a creeping sense of guilt. It irritated him—guilt was not a kingly emotion—and he quelled it as best he could.

After all, the little wretch had thoroughly deserved it.

Still...it would not do to allow enmity between them to linger any longer than was necessary. Puck, for all his failings, was a valuable asset.

Where would he be at this hour of the day? At Oberon's side, usually, discussing matters of state or else attempting to lure him away to more idle pursuits. But otherwise...

It occurred to Oberon that he had very little idea of what Puck did in his spare time.

At the moment, said a small, accusatory voice at the back of his head, *he is likely procuring the ingredients for a healing potion. He will likely be doing so on foot, given that you snapped his wing in two.*

Oberon scowled, and cursed, and went looking for him.

A whole night of fruitless searching later, he stormed back into the throne room just as the sun was peeking over the horizon and was startled to find the ambassadors and his servant engaged in lively conversation.

"Droll, my lord, very droll!" said Puck, his laughter in reaction to one of the ambassador's jokes ringing out like a golden bell.

Oberon approached them slowly; although he was mindful not to allow his discombobulation to show in his step. When they noticed him, all three turned and bowed, although Puck did so more hesitantly. Not a show of defiance, Oberon realised; beneath his leaf shirt, Oberon could see the bandages wrapped across his ribs.

"My lords," said Oberon, returning their bows with a respectful nod. "It pleases my heart to see you. I wanted to offer my apologies for the incident at dinner yesterday."

Before he'd finished the sentence, one of them had made a gesture of dismissal. "Please, mighty Oberon, think nothing of it. A minor accident, nothing more. We have far more important matters to discuss."

"Indeed," said Oberon, his gaze sliding to Puck, who was wearing one of his mysterious smiles. "These trade negotiations..."

✰✰✰

As soon as the ambassadors had departed, Oberon turned on him.

"How did you do it?"

"Do what, master?" Puck inquired, his eyes wide and innocent.

"Don't play with me, sprite. How did you win their favour? I anticipated having to grovel like a cur to make things right."

"Oh, that. What can I say, master? I can be very personable."

Laying a hand on his chest, Puck added, "And I trust my earlier misjudgement is forgiven?"

His wing, Oberon noticed, was also wrapped in bandages.

"Why have you not yet procured a healing potion?" Oberon grunted.

Puck shrugged. "I've not had the time. I wanted to intervene before the situation deteriorated. I have had dealings with Sicinius and Memius in the past; they do like to make mountains out of molehills."

His hand still lay hopeful over Oberon's heart. It fell away as Oberon stepped back and said, "Come. I may have one or two potions lying spare."

Puck thanked him but would not let him apply the healing oils himself. Perturbed, Oberon brooded on the matter for the rest of the day.

All seemed well again that evening when Puck came to him as usual after dinner and kissed him deeply. Later, after they had thoroughly enjoyed one another, Oberon happened to glance down at his back. The potion had worked; the bandages were gone, and both wings fluttered as vigorously as ever.

And on his thin neck, not quite concealed by his thick black curls, there was the red-pink shadow of a love bite Oberon had not put there.

Chapter Four

Oberon hated many things: geese, blisters, rum, ingratitude, and at least a thousand more. Recently, the names Sicinius and Memius had been added to the list. But in all the world, there was nothing Oberon hated more than an unpaid debt.

He thought deeply for many days. How did one reward a servant who prostituted himself to correct what was, in retrospect, a comparatively minor mistake?

And how, said the little voice, *did one apologise for inflicting a punishment that had, in retrospect, been excessive to the point of cruelty?*

Oberon's mind kept returning to the notion of a gift, but while he prized creativity in others, it was not a quality he had in abundance. Try as he might, he was unable to dream up a gift that would please Puck without seeming desperate or trivial.

Then, at long last, an idea occurred.

As Oberon's favourite, Puck had a list of chores and duties longer than any other member of the court.

They ran the gamut from the tedious to the Herculean. Feeding Oberon's pet falcon; perusing his correspondence and sifting out that which was inconsequential; delivering the gossip of the day to his lord's breakfast table; thwarting assassination attempts, of which there were an average of two a week, the fairy court being what it was; and acting as a sounding board for whatever bright governance-related ideas the king had come up with this time, in the hopes of forestalling future assassination attempts.

He guarded each task jealously. Many could easily be handled by someone of lesser wit and ability than he, but Puck plotted out his schedule with meticulous care to ensure that Oberon would never entertain notions of more diverse delegation.

His favourite, by far, was tending to Oberon's hair.

True, his master hardly needed Puck's sartorial attentions to look exquisite. Nor was he a particularly vain creature, at least compared to the rest of their ilk; Titania, for instance, had ten girls constantly on hand whose sole purpose was to polish her wings and primp her tresses. At most, Puck was allowed ten minutes a day to wash, dry, trim, and style Oberon's hair. On special occasions and feast days, he might be allowed fifteen. It was a most wretched business. Were his master not so terribly cruel, he would either give Puck permission to run his fingers through his lovely silver locks at all hours of the day and the night, or forbid his touching them altogether.

"Nothing elaborate," Oberon barked. "I leave on a hunt at first light."

So, that was why his master had hauled him from his bed at an even more unreasonable hour than usual. Hunting was one of Oberon's favourite pastimes, but he rarely had a chance to indulge himself these days, unless he took it into his head to slip away before anyone could object to his departure.

"Your quarry, my liege?" said Puck, putting aside his comb and separating out three thick bundles for a smart but sensible plait. He recalled tales of the badger Oberon had brought home some years ago, whose splendid pelt had been given to Titania. Would Oberon, perhaps, bring him such a gift? If so, it would be well past due. All other highly ranked members of the court showered their retainers and concubines with presents, if only as a means of showing off their wealth to the world. But Puck had received nothing.

"A serpent, I think. Our warriors have need of new armour."

"Then they should hunt it down themselves," muttered Puck, but he knew it was foolish to quibble. Much as he disliked the thought of Oberon heading off into the wilderness alone, he was as strong as twenty fairies, and his agility was the stuff of legend. "Will my master take his bow?"

"No. I am in a mood to kill something with my bare hands."

"As you wish."

He completed the plait, resisting the urge to caress it, and spotting a minor discrepancy, Puck retrieved his silver scissors. He had six pairs, each of a different size, and he cared for them in the way other members of the court cared for their ancestral weaponry.

It would have been well outside the bounds of propriety for Puck to ask if he could come along to watch, but he was disappointed Oberon did not invite him. True, he had little reputation as a hunter, but he knew the wild as well as anyone—better, in fact. He could wind his way through the trees as silently as any ghost and had once followed a mother tiger all the way back to her den without being noticed.

That was when he had an idea.

"What are you smirking about?" Oberon demanded.

"Nothing, my liege. Nothing." Puck stood back, admiring his handiwork. With his hair drawn back, his master's sharp features became distinctly avian.

The lark crowed, and Oberon gave Puck a brisk nod, and an even brisker kiss, before departing.

Fondly, Puck watched him make his way toward the tree line and disappear into the undergrowth. Then he picked up his sharpest scissors and followed him.

☆☆☆

Five hours later, Puck decided his king was significantly cannier than he looked.

His feet were as exhausted as his wings, and he collapsed against a tree root to catch his breath. His stomach growled. He'd had nothing to fill it with all day save for a few sips of dew stolen before it had all evaporated and an overripe berry he'd found on the ground. He'd expected his master to stop for lunch at some point, but Oberon had been on the move all day, never breaking his stride, never seeming to tire.

And now, finally, he'd lost him. He didn't know how it had happened, for he'd barely torn his gaze away from Oberon's broad, muscular back to observe a passing butterfly, and when he'd looked back, he was gone. It was, he supposed, possible that Oberon had sensed his pursuit and turned invisible. He was more than capable of such tricks, for all that he rarely used them.

Drawing his knees up under his chin, Puck set to pouting. It wasn't that he hadn't enjoyed spending the day eyeing his master as he moved through the shadows, his long plait flickering this way and that like the tail of leopard on the prowl. But it had been a lonely business. He'd more than once found himself hoping that Oberon would catch him at it, and administer one of his scoldings.

A noise made his pointed ears twitch, and he scowled at having his sulk interrupted. It came again, and this time, he stood, for it sounded very much like his master shouting, albeit a great distance away. The exact content was indiscernible, but the tone—anger, and fear—was not.

When provided with enough incentive, Puck could move faster than anything alive. It took him barely one minute to scour a square mile's worth of woodland, dispensing with subterfuge entirely in his haste.

Alas, his powers of restraint were not quite as impressive as his swiftness, and upon locating Oberon, the first thing he did was collapse laughing.

"I will gut you like a fish," hissed Oberon, his eyes flaming red. But he was unable to make good the threat due to the huge spider's web, upon which he was stuck.

Clamping a hand over his mouth to stifle the giggles, Puck said, "Forgive me, master. Er...may I be of some assistance?"

He couldn't help but admire him—all laid out, limbs akimbo, hanging several inches above the ground.

"Positively ornamental," Puck said to himself.

"Stop muttering, get up here, and help me, fool," Oberon ordered.

Careful not to touch the sticky strings himself, Puck fluttered up to meet him. His face was flushed, and his plait had come half undone.

"Look at the state of you," Puck murmured, plucking a stray silver strand away from his master's narrowed eyes. "So scruffy. So much for all my hard work."

He wasn't a fool. It hadn't escaped his notice that Oberon could very easily free himself if he wanted to, either with magic or the knife he wore on his belt.

Which meant his master wanted to play.

"You may have to remove my garments to free me," Oberon said in brusque but slightly husky tones, confirming Puck's suspicions.

"Very good, my liege," Puck purred and took out his silver scissors.

He began by cutting away the string that bound what remained of the plait, letting Oberon's hair cascade freely over his shoulders. Delighted at the realisation that, for once, he had all the time in the world, he used his fingers as a comb, to which Oberon rumbled his approval.

Next went Oberon's shirt and belt, and all Puck could think as he devoured the sight of Oberon's bare chest and stomach was *Mine*.

"Must you take all day?" sighed Oberon, feigned annoyance failing to conceal his amusement.

"I'm sorry, master. Am I boring you?" Puck asked sweetly and pinched his nipple. The resultant shout brought an evil grin to his lips, and he leant down to apologise with a lick.

"You are a punishment for my sins," Oberon said, squirming.

Oberon's skin was hot and damp as Puck ran his tongue down his chest. While hoping to remain free of the web himself—unlike

Oberon, he lacked the strength to tear himself loose without assistance—he was able to position his body in such a way as to rest most of his weight against his king, feeling Oberon's cock press against his stomach.

His scissors flashed, and soon he had Oberon entirely naked beneath him.

"Hurry up," Oberon growled, the command undercut by the faintly pleading tone of his voice.

"Patience," Puck said, kissing his navel. His master's cock was impressive, even when soft, and now his fingers strained to wrap around it. When he gave the tip a tiny, kittenish lick, Oberon threw his head back and cursed.

Titania never gives him this, Puck thought. *She never gets to see this. No one does, no one but me.*

Stroking him firmly, Puck raised himself up to lavish attention on Oberon's nipples, which were red and hard as pebbles. With meticulous care, he took one between his teeth, listening to his master's breath hitch.

I don't want anyone else to have him, ever, he realised, watching Oberon bite his lip, his eyes hazy. *Not in all his life. Not if he lives to be twenty thousand years old.*

And behind the thought came another, dark and very clear; *I will happily kill anyone who tries to take this from me.*

When Oberon came, gasping, with the aid of three more firm strokes, Puck followed suit bare seconds afterwards, without having once laid a hand on his cock.

"Why the devil do you have those ridiculous things with you?" Oberon grunted after several minutes of contented silence. Puck's mind was awash with thoughts both pleasant and profane, and it took him a moment to realise that his master was referring to his scissors.

"I prefer them to knives and swords," he told him. "They are far more versatile. And easier to conceal."

"Not a warrior's weapon," said Oberon. "I will have to find you something more suitable."

"A present, master?" asked Puck as he thought, *Tribute. About time.*

"We will see. By the way, you still haven't explained what you were doing following me."

Because I wished to protect my investment. Because I am not some trinket to be left at home when you feel the need for adventure. "Oh...I wanted to watch you hunt, master. They tell such excellent stories of your prowess."

"Do they, indeed."

With ease, Oberon pulled both arms free of the web and folded them around Puck's body. Grunting, he wrenched them both free, tearing the whole sticky construction apart as he did so.

"What would suit you?" Oberon wondered, holding Puck up in his arms and inspecting him. "Not a sword. Not a spear. A bow, perhaps?"

Puck shook his head. "I have little interest in blood sport. Although...you know, master, I have long fancied the idea of a whip."

Oberon's eyes widened slightly, and Puck licked his lips.

"I will speak to our craftsmen," he said, gruffly, pink spots flaring on his cheeks.

"Thank you, sweet master." Puck pressed a feather-light kiss against his chin. "Now, shall we go find your serpent?"

Chapter Five

Having shown Puck the sort of games to which he was partial, Oberon found his servant more than willing to indulge him in the weeks that followed. Puck's appetite was voracious, his creativity unlimited, and Oberon's bed and body soon became testing grounds for his endless fount of new ideas.

This, though...Oberon liked this best.

"Take off your clothing—all your clothing—and turn around so I can have a good look at you," Puck told him.

His sprite sat sprawled in Oberon's throne with his long, tattooed legs hanging over the side, a glass of berry wine in his hand. Oberon stood before him, feeling as exposed and self-conscious as though the room had been filled to capacity. But the doors were locked, and Puck's enchantments would keep prying eyes from the windows. They were, for the next few hours, entirely alone.

Puck's new whip lay idle in his lap, and Oberon couldn't stop looking at it.

He disrobed slowly, proceeding downwards from his thistle crown to his serpent-hide boots. The last were difficult; his fingers felt thick and clumsy, and he fumbled the laces more than once.

When he was naked, he raised himself to his full height, feeling Puck's eyes devouring the sight of his skin and his musculature. The avidness of his servant's gaze made something flutter in his belly, and to his annoyance, he felt himself begin to blush.

"Very good," Puck said, standing and approaching him. He held the whip loosely in his left hand, and as he made a lazy circuit around Oberon's person, he would occasionally let it brush against his side and his thighs. Oberon summoned every last ounce of his considerable willpower and remained utterly still.

It had taken him some time to realise that Puck's public face was little more than an ill-fitting mask, designed to lull those about him into a false sense of security. In public, Puck was light-footed and rarely still, fidgeting constantly and flitting about like a hummingbird. At moments like this, Puck's tread became distinctly panther-like, his mastery of his own body evident in every slow, calculated movement. In public, Puck chattered and babbled and laughed at everything, his white teeth flashing at the slightest provocation. Now, the hard-set lines of his face made him seem as old as Oberon himself, and the only indication of his enjoyment came in the form of small, carnivorous smiles.

"Go and stand next to that table," Puck said, his soft lips brushing the edge of his ear. "Keep your back straight and your head tilted downwards."

Once there, Oberon allowed Puck to position him as he wanted, quavering at the sensation of his neat, delicate hands fluttering from his waist to his thighs, a quiet mutter of approval or discontent accompanying every minor adjustment. Oberon's arms were eventually braced on the tabletop, his legs spread about three feet apart; at the middle, he bent so that his shoulder-length hair fell forward and obscured his view of anything but his own fingers splayed flat upon the table.

Giving himself over as a play thing to Puck's brilliant mind was pleasurable all by itself, but secretly Oberon exulted in the gentle way those hands glided from one part of his body to the next.

"I should have oiled you," Puck sighed, his breath warm on Oberon's back. "These ridiculous muscles of yours...they knot so easily."

Remembrance of the last time Puck had applied one of his exotic lotions to his shoulders and biceps coaxed a soft, shapeless sound from his lips.

Into his ear, Puck hissed, "Yes, you are a complete hedonist, aren't you? You play the mighty unconquered warrior-king so very well. But I think you'd have been just as happy had you been an expensive concubine and spent your life sprawled out on a pile of pillows being fed candied fruits and having your lovely legs massaged, my liege."

A hand cupped his buttocks, squeezed lightly, and then slid round to his cock. One rub was enough to make him leak, whereupon Puck stopped playing and gripped him firmly. Dimly, Oberon was aware that his hips had begun to rock forward.

"Will you take all day, fool?" he snarled, pressing back against Puck's whip-thin body and feeling Puck's erection grinding against him.

Puck snickered at him, sounding drunk, and pushed Oberon's legs further apart before dropping to his knees.

At the first touch of Puck's tongue, Oberon moaned. With effort, he stopped his legs from giving out, but it was a near thing. Everything from the base of his spine downwards felt like overheated steel, warping and melting beneath the warmth of Puck's mouth.

"Mm," Puck grunted, drawing back. "Stop squirming, my liege. You make it very difficult to concentrate."

It was goading. He hadn't been squirming. However, he was in no state to return Puck's parry, with his lover's saliva running down his thigh and his cock now achingly hard. He wanted to touch himself; the only thing he wanted more was to wait until Puck deigned to do it for him. And he had always prided himself on his powers of restraint. So, he bit his lip and felt his face flame with humiliation and feverish need as Puck's tongue lay waste to him.

Finally, his servant drew back and whispered in his ear, "I've not the patience to play with you anymore today. You're too handsome."

"Hurry up," Oberon said; he was capable of nothing else.

Moaning, Puck pressed his face into his back and slowly sank into him. It stung, at first, which was to Oberon's taste. Despite their discrepancy in size, Puck's cock was thick enough to push him just to the point where the pain was delightful without being distracting.

"If ever I find out," Puck said, in the low, fell voice he very occasionally slipped into, "that anyone else has done this to you, anyone, I will find them, Oberon, and I will rip them apart."

"Never," Oberon gasped, all pretence falling away, and how he loved knowing that Puck was the one creature in existence who could strip him down like this. "Only you."

Puck began to synchronise his thrusts with his manipulation of Oberon's cock, bending him further over the table. He had a deep sense of rhythm, and Oberon had often heard him start to hum to himself when they fucked.

"My lord," Puck sighed. "My sweet, fair, lovely lord."

Oberon was beyond words, almost beyond thought. All he could feel was the luscious burn of his lover's cock, and his lover's hands on his hips, and his lover's lips on his back.

Puck took hold of Oberon's hair and wrenched his head back, his other hand gliding up his neck until two of his fingers slipped into Oberon's open mouth. Mewling, Oberon suckled on them as though they were coated in honey and almost wept in protest as they were withdrawn, only to plunge in once more.

"Don't know which end of you I prefer," Puck mumbled.

Two fingers remained in his mouth while Puck's other hand returned to his cock. And surely it must indicate some special show of favour from the gods, that he could have this and Puck whimpering beneath him whenever he wanted it?

Puck never lasted as long as he did—the dubious benefits of youth—and soon gave himself over with a charming little cry. His movements slow with satiation, he then withdrew and forcibly turned Oberon around. Pushing him back onto the table until he lay flat, Puck proceeded to crawl up his front, his hand never once abandoning Oberon's cock.

Oberon had the strangest idea that he was weightless. Puck's face, floating mere inches above him, was so very, very lovely.

"Kiss me," he heard himself plead.

His chest heaved with a quiet sob of gratitude when Puck did. His face felt wet, and when Puck withdrew his lips, he replaced them with his tongue, small and rough, licking away his tears as his palm worked him to completion.

Oberon never made much noise when he came, and today was no exception. It was Puck who moaned when he spilled into his hand, and Oberon took advantage of Puck's distraction to seize him, wrapping both arms around him in a python-tight embrace.

"You are mine," Oberon snarled, locking one leg around both of Puck's—ah, the pleasures of being the larger lover—and curling around him. "Only mine. No one else's, ever."

"Yours," Puck acceded, clinging.

The assurance calmed him. He wasn't sure when it had happened, but somewhere along the line the thought of anyone else having this, having either of them, had become intolerable.

"Mine," Oberon repeated, pressing his nose into Puck's dark hair. His sprite always smelled pleasing after sex.

A strange snuffling sound caught his attention, and he glanced down.

"Why do you weep?" he asked, tilting Puck's head up.

Puck sniffed. His eyes were red, and there was something guilty and miserable behind them.

"It is nothing, my liege," he said. "I weep with happiness; that is all."

It was a lie, an obvious lie, and not for the first time, it occurred to Oberon to wonder how little he knew about his favourite servant. Nonetheless, he was too tired to pursue the matter further, and he fell asleep to the sensation of Puck's lips brushing against his forehead.

☆☆☆

Puck, for his part, did not sleep, not that night, nor for many nights to come. His thoughts were sorely vexed. In the next few days, whenever Oberon did not require his presence, he slunk away to some quiet spot to bury his head in his hands and fret.

I am in love. I am in love.

The mere thought filled him with horror. He considered, many times, leaving the court and disappearing into the wide world. Oberon, of course, would be furious—but that was not what stopped him.

What if Oberon was not only furious, but also grief-stricken? What if he wept, as he'd wept so prettily under Puck's ministrations, and Puck wasn't there to lick his cheeks and comfort him?

I am in love.

How had he let this happen? Was he not Puck, renowned for his guile? Had he not told himself, in no uncertain terms, that Oberon was a means to an end, a useful, powerful fool, of the sort he was accustomed to playing with? But how could he have known that Oberon would have a gentle heart, and that he'd let Puck wrap his devious little fingers around it so readily? How could he have known Oberon would smell like warm grass in midsummer, and that his lips would be soft?

Puck groaned and beat his head against the wall of the cave in which he had secluded himself.

When Oberon next saw him, his obvious concern for the large red welt on Puck's forehead made Puck's heart lurch in a most disconcerting fashion.

I am in love. And so is he.

Oh, damn.

Chapter Six

With love came jealousy.

It had not escaped eagle-eyed Puck's notice that half the court was infatuated with his master. Whenever Oberon went down to the river to bathe, the surrounding bushes and the branches overhead would bristle with spies, drinking in the sight of water trickling down his strong thighs. On those occasions when there were ambassadors to be greeted and Puck was given free rein to dress Oberon up in such a way as to show off his beauty to the fullest, soft sighs would echo from every corner of the throne room.

What was so infuriating was that Oberon didn't seem to notice. He stalked amongst his subjects convinced they did his bidding out of fear or loyalty to his house, totally oblivious to all the longing, cow-eyed stares.

Every single one of them would happily drop to their knees the moment you asked it of them, my sweet, stupid king.

With jealousy came fear. Granted, Oberon's fascination with him had in no way declined, but lasting monogamy was a rare, rare thing amongst immortals such as they.

What could he do to cement his place in Oberon's affections? Was there something he could give him that no one else could? Wit, yes; charm, yes; resourcefulness, yes; he had all those. But so did many of the simpering creatures who surrounded his master on a daily basis—although Puck flattered himself that he had said qualities in uncommonly even proportion, and that he conducted himself with more dignity than most.

But there had to be something...

Hmm. His master had a taste for pain. Perhaps he'd appreciate a partner who shared his proclivities? After all, Puck didn't mind pain, not that much. Not in small doses. And he was always up for new experiences.

Yes, he'd do it.

☆☆☆

When Puck had first made the suggestion, Oberon had been taken aback. He'd been disinclined, at first, but the notion had grown in his mind like a weed, and ultimately—of course—he had consented.

"Punish me," Puck whined. "Punish me, master, I want...oh..."

"Oh, shush. You're distracting me."

"I want to be your slave, master."

"You want no such thing," Oberon replied, clicking his tongue in disgust. "Crass, self-indulgent creature."

The next time the lash fell, Puck's cry was ear-splitting. Oberon did not pretend that playing the enraged regent was not an appealing change of pace, nor that Puck did not make a lovely sight, arms up, wrists bound, grinding his thin body against the pole to which he had been tied.

"Shameless wretch," Oberon intoned, no longer able to resist the urge to step forward and press his front against Puck's back. His prisoner's breath was shaky and uneven as Oberon's claws curved across his torso in a proprietary fashion.

"I do," Puck said, softly. "Provided I wouldn't have to share you with anyone."

For a moment, Oberon went still before resuming his caresses. "Titania has no part of me."

"I know. I do know."

"Then who..."

A shrug of those narrow shoulders. "You are our king. You belong to everyone. I would it were otherwise."

Teasing now, Oberon nipped at the tip of his ear. "What can I do to show my lover how I prize him? Some bauble, perhaps? A crown? A palace of your own? An army? Or perhaps I should just drape my pet in as many gold chains and silver necklaces as his lovely form would accommodate..."

As he knew he would—and it was priceless, to know that only he was permitted to play upon him this way—Puck reared up, hissing. "You insult me! Take your trinkets and choke on them, tyrant! This pet will have nothing from you!"

Oberon snarled in approval and brought the lash down again. "Except this! You'll have no end of this, won't you? You'll accept all the blows and indignities I have to offer!"

Puck moaned brokenly.

"And the responsibilities," Oberon continued, one lash following another, and another. "And every demeaning task I can think to heap upon your shoulders. So much I have to offer you, yet all that interests you is the chaff."

He was, he realised, enjoying this a great deal. A wash of affection came over him; his sprite had a way of opening his eyes to new pleasures.

Finally tiring, he set the whip aside. Folding his arms around Puck, he pressed his cock into the cleft of his attractive little arse. In the secret depths of his heart, he would very much have liked to sink into him and fuck him raw, but they had never broached the subject, and he was mindful of his size. He satisfied himself as best he could with their closeness and the smell of his servant's blood.

Later, while he was rubbing balm over Puck's wounds, he caught him looking pensive. It was an off look, one that seemed unnatural on a face where dozens of expressions flickered like a candle in a strong breeze even when the sprite did nothing more than stand, immersed in thought.

"What is it?"

"Hmm? Oh...nothing, master. Mm, rub there again."

✩✩✩

Puck was unsatisfied.

Well, no, that wasn't quite right. While he still hadn't succeeded in cultivating a taste for pain, the luxury of having his master's undivided attention was satisfying in and of itself. Still, he wanted more.

He needed to think bigger. Some great gift, some grand gesture that would ensure that Oberon's heart would remain in his keeping until the stars went dark.

When, at last, an idea came to him, he threw back his head and cackled.

Chapter Seven

"Sprite!"

A long ribbon of lightning crossed the sky at the sound of Oberon's voice. Insects scuttled for the safety of the undergrowth, and birds took flight all over the forest. Fire flickering in his hair and poisons sweating from the soles of his feet, the fairy king left a trail of burnt branches and wilted flowers in his wake as he sought out his servant.

"Lazy, useless, erratic..."

Spitting invective with every step, he had scoured the grove where the rest of his court were playing mouse polo, and the canopy where Titania and her entourage retreated to discuss serious matters, and the spot behind the waterfall where restless spirits lurked. Six hours, now, he'd been searching, his mood growing fouler with every passing minute. As a result, a sky which had been as blue as a robin's egg this morning was now as grey and damp as a freshly unearthed corpse.

"Sprite! Puck!"

A growl of thunder was the only response. He bit his lip in frustration, piercing it with one of his shark-like teeth.

It was not that Puck's absences were an infrequent occurrence. Now and then, he would simply disappear, fluttering off into the wide world and returning to Oberon's side a day later with a guilty expression and, often, a new trinket or set of scars. But this was different. Of late, it seemed as though every time Oberon looked about for his most-prized servant—to assign him a new task, or to cuff him for failing to complete one already assigned—he was nowhere to be found.

Is it possible Puck has found something more interesting than his master's company? The thought made Oberon's teeth grind and his heart ache quietly.

He had, of course, a great many other servants. But none had Puck's wit, nor his smooth skin, nor his insolent little smirk that just begged to be slapped off his face. So it was that Oberon had endured the last four nights alone, curled on his side with his fists clenched and his jaw locked in frustration and misery.

The worst of it was that he'd begun to have dreams. They were ephemeral things, with no logical progression; one moment he'd be hanging, weightless, between the stars and the ocean's surface, and the next moment slim, strong fingers would grasp his ankles and drag him down like an anchor to the ocean depths, where everything was dark, and all he could see were bright black eyes, laughing at him. Invariably, he would wake up before anything remotely like satisfaction could be achieved and find himself sweat soaked and skin starved. After the first two nights, he'd grown weary of his own touch and tried to will his body into behaving itself.

It had not worked. Today, he'd been forced to receive those who prostrated themselves before his throne from a slouched position that made his back ache, just to conceal the extent to which it had not worked.

"Sprite! Reveal yourself at once!"

Now hoarse from shouting, Oberon paced the forest floor, cursing all that lived under his breath. At length, he made a decision. It was unprecedented, and well below his dignity, but he saw no alternative.

Puck made his home some way away from the rest of the court, in a hole a woodpecker had carved in the bough of a stout willow. Oberon had never before visited—why should he? Most kings, he thought peevishly, did not have to leave the comfort of their thrones in order to converse with those who purportedly served them. Nevertheless, he knew where to find it, and picking apart the protective wards that guarded the entrance was the work of seconds.

The interior was far more orderly than he would have expected. A handsome shrew-skin rug, upon which sat several tidily arranged pieces of stick furniture, painted red with berry juice. A bed of daisy and tulip petals, with a ball of duckling feathers for a pillow. A collection of oddments lining the walls; dead beetles bound with string, several rose-coloured pebbles of varying sizes, and what looked very much like the skull of a toad.

And a complete absence of Puck. Briefly, Oberon considered setting fire to the willow, out of sheer spite.

Then his gaze fell upon the acorn-shell that served as a table. A small pile of parchment scraps sat atop it, bearing the almost indecipherable scrawl he recognised as Puck's own hand. Hoping for some clue as to its owner's whereabouts, he lifted the first piece and read it slowly.

Then, with his pupils inflated and his lips parted, he read it again. And again.

Chapter Eight

The weather was foul, and Puck returned to his home in the willow tree with his wings soaked and his mood thoroughly rotten. He bore over one shoulder a bottle full of ink pilfered from a mortal aristocrat's desk, and over the other, a basket full of rose thorns that could be fashioned into adequate writing tools. Both were heavy, and he'd carried them many miles. Now, he wanted nothing more than to retrieve the thimbleful of purple pansy wine he had hidden somewhere deep in his den and sulk for the rest of the evening.

It pleased him not, therefore, to find Oberon seated at his acorn-shell table, in his favourite chair, leafing through his private correspondence. He had, Puck noted, left a trail of poisonous footprints all over his favourite rug. Lovely.

"This day has been a hurricane of shit, and I am not in the mood to talk to you," Puck grumbled as he shook the rain from his black curls. Dropping both bottle and basket in a corner, he went in search of his wine.

Oberon said nothing but continued to read the piece of parchment to which his gaze was affixed.

Puck, for his part, drank until his belly was full and then flopped onto his petal bed and reflected bleakly upon his woes. When he became bored with the enterprise, he returned his attention to his guest. Oberon looked strangely dishevelled. His thistle crown was nowhere to be seen; his cape of swallow feathers had been discarded on the floor; his long silver hair was loose and damp, spread unevenly across his broad shoulders.

The sight of him, at once shining and rock solid, did something to soothe Puck's many grievances.

"Master, what are you doing here?" he said, in more conciliatory tones.

Quietly, Oberon said, "Did you write these?"

"What? What are you reading?"

Swinging his legs off the bed, Puck came to his feet with less grace than was his wont, his still-damp wings setting him off balance. Fluttering away the lingering droplets, he made his way to Oberon's side and stood on the tips of his toes to peer over the king's huge shoulder.

"What are you doing?" he shrieked and lunged for the piece of parchment clasped in Oberon's hand. Oberon shook him off and pushed him back onto the floor with an irritated grunt, and without removing his eyes from the page.

Getting to his feet, he said, "That is mine, Oberon, you have no right..."

"Did you write them?" Oberon barked. "Are they yours?"

Puck paused and reassessed Oberon's expression. While the usual background noise of impatience, imperiousness, and irritation were all present in Oberon's face at that moment, there was something else.

Lust?

"Er," Puck said, annoyed to find himself wrong-footed. "I...yes. I did. But they're not finished. You shouldn't read them until I've made them perfect."

Oberon continued to stare at him in that unsettlingly intent way. All at once, he got to his feet. Puck instinctively retreated a step, mindful of his master's mercurial moods, and his own recent unauthorised absence.

"This one," Oberon said, thrusting the parchment at Puck as though it were a blade. There was, Puck noticed for the first time, a spot of dried blood on the edge of his lower lip. "Its shape differs from the others."

"What? Oh...that one. I was experimenting with form," Puck replied, adrift in what was rapidly mutating into one of the more bizarre conversations of his very long life.

"Read it," Oberon ordered, folding his arms across his chest. "Out loud. Now."

The experience was mortifying. Even if it hadn't been unfinished, trailing away into nothing at the end, there were at least three segments that just didn't sound right, and the overall tone was dreadfully maudlin. Not one of his better pieces, although he kept coming back to it in the hope that one more minor adjustment might pull the whole thing together. It was also noticeably lacking in innuendo; he'd been in an odd mood when he'd first jotted it down. If he'd had to choose a poem to present to Oberon, it would have been one of his cleverly obscene triolets.

When he finished, he looked at Oberon's expression again and found that his eyes were hooded and his pupils wide.

"My lord?" he said timidly.

Oberon cleared his throat, but there was still a noticeable husk in his voice when he said, "Who is William?"

He thrust forward another piece of parchment, this time drawing Puck's attention to the words "For Dear William" scrawled at the bottom of the poem in his own minute handwriting. Ah.

Puck winced. "Er. Well..."

"Is he your lover?" Oberon pressed with poorly suppressed covetousness.

"No, no! He is a mortal. A friend."

A growl from deep within Oberon's chest seemed to make the entire forest shudder. "You abandon my court for days on end to consort with some blasted mortal, in blatant disregard of my laws?"

"My king, you don't understand. He is not like the rest of them. He's special."

Now the clouds of jealousy had thoroughly settled on his master's face, along with just a touch of hurt. "Special, is he? And what is it that distinguishes him from the rest of his wretched ilk? Does he have golden scales? Can he make the world spin backwards when he sneezes? Can he fell a giant in a single blow?"

"He is an artist." It occurred to Puck that there was a very easy way to slide young William into Oberon's graces. "And he is writing a play about you."

"Is he, indeed?" said Oberon, evidently unimpressed. "And what in Persephone's name is a 'play'?"

Puck sighed internally. His master was terribly provincial sometimes. "It's a bit like a story and a bit like a dance. Men pretend to be women, mortals pretend to be immortal. They wear colourful costumes and stab one another with imaginary swords. Usually, someone either falls in love or dies, and very often, there are rude jokes."

"I see." Oberon's anger seemed to have abated somewhat, though a shadow still lingered on his brow. "And for what confounded reason is this William writing a play about me?"

"Oh, but who wouldn't want to write a play about my most excellent master?" Puck said with as much charm as he could muster.

Oberon's flat, stony expression suggested that it hadn't worked.

"I bribed him," Puck admitted.

"With what?" said Oberon sharply. Clearly, he had not forgotten the time when Puck had attempted to bribe a nymph into handing over her flute by offering her a ray of light from the moon. Nighttimes all over the world had been plunged into pitch-black gloom for weeks until Oberon had throttled him into rescinding the offer.

"With these," said Puck, gesturing to the bits of parchment. "He has a woman he wants to woo and to win. I promised him that if he devised a play about us—about you, that is—I would write him a poem so beautiful that her heart would all but break for love of him."

"You have succeeded," Oberon muttered, returning his gaze to the poem in his hand.

"Oh, no, that's only a draft. It's not nearly finished yet. I've been working on it for weeks now, but I just can't seem to get it right..."

When Oberon didn't reply, Puck took a hesitant step forward, his shoulders hunched. "I am sorry for my absence, master. But procuring writing materials has consumed almost all of my time.

That, and William often asks for stories of your court, and you know how much I appreciate a good listener. I think you would like him too, if you met him."

"Hmph. And you want him to write a play about me. Why?"

Embarrassed, Puck shifted from foot to foot. "I have seen many of his other plays. Most of them feature renowned mortal rulers—kings, princes, dukes, and lords. The subject of leadership clearly fascinates him. I thought it absurd that he should waste his creative energies recounting the exploits of such trifling people, and write nothing of the greatest king in all the world."

For a while, there was silence, but for the pattering of the rain outside.

"How?" Oberon murmured, still staring at the parchment. "How do you do it? How do you make these?"

"Oh...I've not really thought about it. I think of lines and stanzas while I fly and tie them together when I lie awake in the small hours."

"You compose while you fly," Oberon said, looking his way at last. His dark red eyes had taken on a strange gleam, like a feral cat on the prowl for dinner. "How very appropriate."

"Are you well, my lord?" Puck squeaked as Oberon loomed over him (and yes, all right, maybe he'd always quite liked it when Oberon did that, on a purely aesthetic level. Oberon looked his best from below).

"I am very well, Puck," Oberon purred, leaning down. In order to be at eye level with his servant, he had to make himself almost perpendicular.

"Um," Puck said, as the tip of Oberon's finger pressed into the underside of his chin and stroked it gently.

"I simply had no idea that we had a poet in our midst," he said into Puck's pointed ear, his other hand appearing at the edge of Puck's left wing and playfully flicking at it.

"Can I take it that you like my poetry?" Puck managed, although the urge to lean forward and let Oberon's powerful presence envelop him whole was strong.

Oberon snickered darkly. "I imagine you can. You're usually quite good at taking it."

"Master!" Puck said, as though scandalised rather than delighted.

With one arm, Oberon swept clear the tabletop, sending parchments fluttering through the air like butterflies. Then, as though he weighed nothing at all, he lifted Puck up onto it, holding him in place with his hands on Puck's hips.

"Make me a poem, my sprite, and I'll kiss you," said the king, his eyes now feverishly bright.

Winding both arms around his neck and ducking his head to take in the storm scent of his hair, Puck said, "An entire poem, all for you? That's a lot of work for one kiss."

"Opportunist!" Oberon snarled. "What would satisfy you, then?"

A world of dizzying possibilities opening up before him, Puck curbed the desire to reply, *Conclude your barren farce of a marriage and promise that I will always be your favourite.* Instead, he said, "Well, I suppose you could surrender leadership of the fairy tribes to me and accept your immediate demotion to the position of my consort and plaything."

For an instant, it looked alarmingly as though Oberon were seriously considering it. Hurriedly, Puck added, "But in lieu of that, I am willing to accept a kiss per line."

At that, Oberon grinned his cruellest grin and licked his lips. Puck could admit that Oberon, for his all faults—pig-headedness, meanness of spirit, a terrible taste in wives—had never been anything less than breathtakingly beautiful. There was a particularly embarrassing ode he'd written—now locked away in an enchanted box and resting at the bottom of the ocean—on the subject of Oberon's thighs. He'd been outrageously drunk at the time, and the end result had been monstrous. He'd used the word "magnificent" three times, and at one point compared him to an ancient sea monster. But what had infuriated Puck, upon reading it sober, had not been the inelegance of its construction, but the fact that it failed utterly to convey poetically even an ounce of Oberon's true splendour.

Said splendour, particularly at close range, had a tendency to reduce Puck's silver tongue to babbling.

"What...what would you prefer, my lord? In terms of form? A trochaic? A limerick? I-I have recently begun experimenting with a foreign art called haiku..."

"What is the one you are composing for your mortal friend called again?"

"A sonnet."

"Then I want a sonnet too. And it must be better than his."

"But master, I have been working on his for weeks!"

"Then let me incentivise you," said Oberon, one of his large hands sliding up Puck's thigh, and underneath his skirt of honey-coloured moth wings.

Never let it be said that Puck did not know how to work under pressure. Biting his lip to hold back a moan, he scanned his memory for lines and fragments he'd discarded over the course of the last few weeks. Most were dross, but here and there, he found flickers of potential, and he cobbled them together as best he could as Oberon's thumb rubbed teasingly over his skin, bare micrometres from his cock.

"Stop, stop," he said, shifting backwards. "I need to concentrate. Ah. All right. Listen:

Lord of my love, to whom in vassalage
Thy merit hath my duty strongly knit
To thee I send this written ambassage
To witness duty, not to show my wit..."

He deployed his richest voice, the one that could charm mermaids, to disguise the haste of its construction, and the hesitancy of his recital. Going by the way Oberon's breathing had grown shallow and swift, it was working.

"...Till whatsoever star that guides my moving
Points on me graciously with fair aspect

And puts apparel on my tottered loving
To show me worthy of their sweet respect..."

"Fuck," Oberon rasped as he finished, and Puck, who had never once heard him swear, suddenly wanted nothing more than to hear it a second time.

"Master, you promised. My kisses?"

Oberon's mouth was hot and cruel and sweet all at once. The feel of his shark-like teeth pricking at his tongue was incomparable.

And...Hecate's tits. Showers of golden fairy dust had begun to cascade from Puck's skin. How embarrassing.

"I love it when you creatures do that," Oberon rumbled before resuming his kiss. His strong fingers came to rest upon Puck's sensitive gossamer wings, his touch deceptively light as he ran them up and down, almost as though he were playing an instrument.

The desire to please his king was suddenly viciously potent.

Oberon grunted in surprise as Puck dropped to his knees, landing in a small pile of golden dust, and set his nimble fingers to work undoing the clasp on his master's lizard-skin belt (oh, oh, he was hard, he was leaking). When Oberon's cock was released, he fondled it for moment and sighed as he felt Oberon's rough hand slide deep into his hair.

"Puck," Oberon rumbled in approval, the sound of his rich, textured voice sinking into Puck's bones like hot oils rubbed onto his skin.

It fired his will. Concentrating, he sucked Oberon's cock down into his throat. The subsequent hoarse shout, and the awareness that this was as deep as he'd ever taken him before, prompted him to congratulate himself and to set to one side the fact that he was very much in need of air. When, a moment later, his vision began to blur, he assumed it was because tears of joy had gathered in his eyes, and he blinked to clear them. When that didn't work and he registered the burning pain in his chest, he had enough time to think *Oh, damn.*

"Puck?"

Drawing on what strength he had left, he braced his hands on

Oberon's thighs (oh, oh, they were as solid as tree trunks, so beautiful...no, concentrate, concentrate) and pushed himself back until Oberon's cock slid from his mouth, and he gasped. After sucking down half a dozen much-welcome lungfuls of air, he glanced up to see Oberon glaring down at him.

"Sprite, did you actually almost suffocate yourself fellating me?"

Sheepishly, he said, "Apologies," and offered Oberon's cock a few conciliatory licks.

To his delight, moist droplets wet his tongue, and he suckled on the tip as Oberon fell back against the wall, moaning.

"Master," he said and found himself wrenched from his knees, his feet leaving the floor entirely as Oberon scooped him up into the cradle of his arms. His wings were practically vibrating now, and the sound that left his mouth as Oberon pressed kisses against his areola was unguarded and embarrassingly loud.

"What do you want? Tell me, sprite."

"Anything, master, please."

Their cocks were pressed together now, rubbing firmly, and he blushed in awareness of how much bigger his master was.

Ah. Now, there was a thought. They'd never tried it before—he'd been too shy to ask, and Oberon had never offered—but you only lived once...

"Master, would you like to..." Hoping to avoid having to actually say the words, he crammed as much insinuation into his voice and his eyebrows as was possible.

"To what? Spit it out."

Puck squirmed, which, given the circumstances, did nothing to aid his concentration. "Would you like to have me in the manner in which...wolves and lions and other brave kings of nature have their mates?"

Licking his reddened nipple, Oberon replied in honey-sweet tones, "I fear that I lack your mastery of wordplay, dear Puck. You will have to speak plainly."

Glaring at him, Puck ground out, "Would my good and most

gracious lord care to fuck me?"

Oberon snorted. "For a poet, your grasp of eroticism leaves something to be desired. But as you ask; I would indeed."

He turned him around (manhandled him, mmm, yessssss) and pressed him against the moss-coated wall of his home, feeling the heat of his huge chest and the beating of the powerful heart against his back. He seemed to fill the entire world, his hair spilling over to lie soft as silk on Puck's dust-coated shoulders.

"Although," Oberon added, low and wicked, "if your infamously capacious mouth was too small to accommodate me without your nearly choking to death, I do wonder whether the rest of you is up to the task."

"Fear not, master," Puck purred. "I welcome a challenge. And I've been... *practicing* in my spare moments."

Oberon snarled, his nails digging trenches in his shoulders, making him cry out in pleasure. The lash, it was true, had done little to rouse him, but this...this was different, somehow.

"Yes, I imagine you have," Oberon hissed in his ear. "You've always had a perverse love of being pushed past your meagre limits. In all likelihood you've let half the court have their way with you."

They both knew full well that Puck had had no other lovers, and that all his practicing had been with his own fingers and a few toys. Mock-jealousy was part of the game.

"I imagine you like them big. You probably don't even prepare yourself," Oberon continued. "Just let them—nngh—make you bleed. Is that what you like, my Puck?"

His cock felt wonderful pressed into the small of Puck's back, thick and hot, and yes, Puck did, indeed, like them big. That said...

"I do...ah...I do like some preparation, master."

Immediately, Oberon stripped him, pulling away his skirt, and slowly slid his fingers down his cleft. Puck indulged himself in a memory of the time he'd watched those fingers tear open the throat of a mortal hunting dog who had invaded the Court's territory in an effort to catch one of his pet foxes. Oberon was not, by nature, a gentle creature, and there was something very touching in all his attempts to simulate tenderness.

At the feeling of Oberon's fingers pressing into him, Puck moaned, fluttering frantically. The stretch, the burn of them would have satisfied him very well had he not known what else was on offer.

"Pretty bird," Oberon husked. "Is that enough?"

With difficulty, Puck mustered a smirk. "Impatient, are we?"

Oberon's free hand slapped his rear, hard. Even he seemed startled by the wanton moan this tore from Puck's mouth.

"Oh, fuck, do that again, master, please."

The next slap was harder, and Puck's knees buckled. He would have collapsed had Oberon not caught him at the waist and dragged him back against his chest.

"Now," Puck said, his tongue feeling thick and stupid even as his head felt feather-light.

Oberon entered him all the way, in one thrust. It felt as though he was being split apart. His head fell back and lolled blissfully against Oberon's damp chest, feeling it rumble, enjoying the way it rose and sank.

He opened his eyes, found Oberon peering down at him, and regretted that their angle was such that leaning in for a kiss would strain his neck. So instead, he clenched and watched his master's changing expression. The rest of court would not have recognised him, so accustomed were they to seeing him frowning, or moping, or smirking in anticipation of a foe's imminent demise. But he wore none so well as the look of pure bliss that flickered across his handsome face as Puck pressed back against him.

Puck had all but forgotten about his own body, and it reminded him of its presence with a sharp throb. But when he reached for it, he found his hand batted away, and Oberon's wide palm slid over his shaft.

"Oberon," he sighed, as a thrust sent his whole body rocking forward, forcing his cock through the tunnel of Oberon's hand.

"My Puck," Oberon returned, sounding, gratifyingly, almost as love-drunk as he did. Puck craned his head back and nuzzled Oberon's neck with his nose, shuddering as Oberon squeezed gently.

"Master, don't tease."

"'Don't tease', my seducer says, as his beautiful body takes me to the hilt," Oberon muttered. "'Don't tease', indeed. Very well. Have what you want, then, most impudent servant."

He began to thrust deep and quick, each one sending Puck forward into his hand and punching a gasp from his mouth. It hurt, and he suspected he'd be bleeding by the end of it. The thought made him mewl.

Perhaps Oberon had a point regarding his perversity.

When Oberon came, clutching him so hard he felt his bones grind together, Puck smiled victoriously at having outlasted him. The next moment, Oberon's huge hand struck him once again, and he lost himself entirely.

"Oh, that will leave a bruise," he crooned as he came back to the world. "Hopefully in the shape of a handprint. Heh."

"Is there no end to your deviance?" Oberon said, sighing heavily. He gave his cock a final squeeze before releasing it and turning Puck round to face him. The flush that adorned his face lent it a softness that Puck found he liked. And now, his lips were perfectly positioned for that kiss.

Taking hold of a lock of silver hair and using it to drag him down, Puck thought of a conclusion to his rapidly assembled sonnet. He sang it into Oberon's ear:

"Then may I dare to boast how I do love thee

Till then, not show my head where thou mayst prove me."

When, at length, the king and his servant emerged from the willow, it was to a fresh and cloudless night.

☆☆☆

"...Think but this, and all is mended..."

Invisible to mortal eyes, they watched William's new play draw to a close from the safety of an abandoned bird's nest tucked away at the top of the theatre.

"Adequate," said Oberon. "Although the bits with the donkey seemed unnecessarily vulgar. We must ensure that Titania never hears of it, else she will set the entire mortal realm to the torch."

"I liked the fellow who played me," said Puck as he curled up in Oberon's lap, his arm thrown loosely around his waist.

"Did you? I considered him to be the low point."

In retribution, Puck bit his arm. Oberon lay a kiss on his wing and continued: "As might be expected. Any mere copy would seem tawdry and plain in the face of so striking an original."

"Better, master," said Puck, settling back against Oberon's chest to watch the mortals take a bow.

Midsummer Sky

Chapter One

"*Ugh*, this heat. All ten thousand bellows in Hephaestus's forge are being worked today."

"Quiet, fool. You made me miss my shot," Oberon growled as another arrow fell short of the mark.

Puck pouted and returned his attention to the sky.

The problem was that Oberon had now missed his shot three times in a row, largely because he couldn't stop looking Puck's way. His servant was remarkably fetching, perched on the edge of the cliff overlooking their valley, his long legs dangling over the side.

The last few days had been intensely humid—as though Puck needed an excuse to scamper about with practically nothing on—and he was fanning himself with a goose feather while sweat trickled down his back. His only concession to decency was a strip of white silk, pilfered from a lady's handkerchief on one of his jaunts to the mortal world, now wrapped loosely around his hips. It left most of his lovely arse exposed and concealed just enough of his groin to tantalise the eye.

He had thoroughly ensnared Oberon's attention for the last half hour.

"Nearly, master," he called encouragingly as Oberon missed again.

Puck's ostensible reason for being there was to gather herbs that didn't grow in the valley below, although his basket now sat abandoned as he took in the view. Oberon's ostensible reason for joining him was to shoot down a swallow or two, in order to present Titania with fresh feathers to adorn her cape.

That, at least, was the excuse Titania had been kind enough to provide him with, being fully aware her husband very much liked swallow meat, and very much liked having a reason to get away from the court for a few days with his servant at his side. He'd brought his best bow, his best knife, and provisions to last them five days.

However, at the moment, Oberon's heart wasn't in hunting. The sky was perfectly blue, and although it was hot, there was a strong breeze blowing up from the valley. What he really wanted was to step off the edge of the cliff and fly up into the open air.

He smirked and thought, *If only*.

"Master?"

As ever, Puck displayed a remarkable talent for detecting changes in his mood. He'd lowered the feather and gazed up at Oberon with his eyes wide and anxious. His lips were parted—the heat making him pant—and his skin was glossy.

Gloomy thoughts temporarily set aside, Oberon felt his body stir. He rubbed his chin and observed with satisfaction the way Puck's eyes meandered up his legs. Because most fairies flew as often as they walked, the pronounced musculature of Oberon's thighs was uncommon, and today, it was on display. This far from court, he'd felt comfortable abandoning all but the essentials: a loincloth cut from a lily pad, affording the bare minimum of modesty, and a necklace of vole teeth, enchanted to keep mosquitoes at bay.

"Yes, my servant?" he replied, deploying the rich purr that always reduced Puck's witty mind to porridge.

"Um..." Puck faltered. His wings had begun to flutter in excitement, the bright sunlight painting them honey gold and making their intricate patterns shimmer. Oberon felt a flicker of envy, but it passed quickly, an inferno of lust taking its place. He reached for him, only to have light-footed Puck duck to one side and spring to his feet, giggling. Exasperated, Oberon reached a second time, and again Puck slid out of his arms gracefully, provoking a growl. The third time, Puck evaded Oberon's grasp by leaping into the air, his wings becoming a blur, but Oberon took hold of his ankle with one hand and prepared to tug him back down.

To Oberon's surprise, however, he found that it was he who was tugged upward, until only his toes touched the ground.

"Your wings are strong," he admitted grudgingly.

Puck preened. "I take good care of them. Unlike some I could name."

Unlike all other members of Oberon's court, Puck approached the subject of his master's disability with a staggering lack of delicacy and tact. When he'd learned no one knew exactly how Oberon's wings had been lost, he'd made a game out of guessing. Every time he guessed incorrectly, he allowed Oberon to give his rear a smack. Needless to say, Puck's guesses tended to be ludicrous. Recently, he'd suggested Oberon had simply neglected his poor wings to such an extent that one day they'd fallen off and been carried away by a badger.

Unfortunately, at that moment Puck's rear was just out of smacking range. Desiring it closer, and unwilling to lose the tug-of-war, Oberon wrapped both hands around the lovely ankle and pulled down as hard as he could. Naturally, that was precisely the moment Puck stopped fighting him. The end result was that they both went sprawling back onto the rock.

"Brute," said Puck, now splayed across Oberon's chest.

"Silly thing," Oberon scolded, burying his nose in Puck's curly black hair. It was even more unruly than usual, as he'd been growing it out in preparation for the festival next month.

Once again, Oberon noticed Puck's wings catching the morning light as they flicked this way and that. Fascinated, he touched the edge of one with his fingertip, and felt his servant shiver.

"*Mmm.* What are you up to, my liege?"

It had been years—centuries—since Oberon had had wings of his own, but he remembered well how wonderfully sensitive they'd been. Bringing the rest of his fingertips into play and locking Puck in place with one strong leg so he couldn't squirm away, he set out to determine whether his servant shared his lost weakness. The results were promising; within several minutes of his tickling and teasing them, Puck's wings had showered them both in fairy dust, and Puck was rubbing against his leg.

"Master," he gasped, clutching a handful of Oberon's silver hair, as he was wont to do on occasions when he forgot himself.

Oberon had always liked the way Puck's cock fit in his hand, as though it had been made for it. As he stroked him, he continued his tactile inspection of Puck's wings, now interested in the spot where they met with his lean back.

Licking the sweat from Oberon's collarbone, Puck said, "Did you know, my liege, some mortals believe that eagles mate in flight?"

"In flight? Preposterous. How do mortals come by these strange ideas?"

"Well, to be fair, mortal eyes are weak. From the ground, the courtship rituals birds of prey perform can look rather like mating. Tumbling through the sky, talons clasping, feathers flared. It's splendidly erotic."

Oberon paused his ministrations and said, with narrowed eyes, "What are you getting at, sprite?"

With a mischievous smile, Puck wriggled out of Oberon's grip. Distressed, Oberon tried to snatch him, but once again, the sprite took to the air—only this time, he held out a hand towards Oberon.

"Shall we, master?" he asked.

Catching on, Oberon looked at him doubtfully. "I'm almost exactly twice as large as you."

"As you yourself observed, my wings are strong."

Oberon still had reservations. However, it was known throughout the land that when Puck came up with novel ideas, whether they pertained to royal policy or loveplay, Oberon tended to indulge his experimentation. This was partly because most of Puck's ideas produced positive results, or else failed in such a way as to provide new knowledge. It was also partly due to the fact that Oberon was prey to a haunting fear that someday his servant would grow to find him dull.

Puck's mind was a glittering jewel, his appetite for new experiences unquenchable. And Oberon, while confident in his abilities to govern his people and defend his court from its enemies, was aware he lacked imagination, knew little of the mortal world Puck found so endlessly fascinating, and rarely attempted new things unless encouraged.

So he extended his arm and allowed Puck's gracile fingers to interlock with his. "If you drop me, I will hunt you to the end of the earth."

Reservations aside, he couldn't deny the powerful joy that overcame him as his feet left the ground.

"Hold on tight, master," Puck said, allowing Oberon to take hold of him firmly. He took them over the cliff edge, out into the warm wind, and Oberon was disgusted with himself when his stomach churned at the realization of just how high up they were. He could see to the very edges of his kingdom, the snow-capped mountains in the west, and when Puck took them higher still, the river that bisected their valley became as thin as a strand of hair. But Puck showed no sign of strain. Presumably, he was using some sort of enchantment to lessen Oberon's weight, for Oberon found he didn't even have to hold on that tight.

Didn't have to, but did. Puck was still hard, and this close, he smelt perfectly edible.

"A-aah! Master, if you keep that up, I *will* drop you."

"Then you'll just have to catch me again, won't you?" Oberon replied and continued in his endeavours to *keep it up*, as it were. After a moment spent palming his servant's arse, he tore away the skimpy strip of silk and let it fly off on the wind.

He groaned in approval as Puck's long, slender legs wrapped around his waist. Being buffeted by the warm breeze and entirely at Puck's mercy made every inch of him ache with want, and he began to contemplate the carnal potential of their current position.

He didn't see the eagle until it was too late.

☆☆☆

Oberon woke to the smell of bird shit. Head throbbing, he rolled onto his back and shielded his eyes from the sun. It was midday—he'd been unconscious for less than an hour. Sitting up, he surveyed a landscape of twigs, feathers, and yes, bird shit. An eagle's nest.

But no eagle in sight, nor any hungry chicks. Nor, for that matter, his bow. It must have fallen to the forest floor. The attack had come out of nowhere. One moment he'd had Puck in his arms, the next moment he'd caught a glimpse of clasping talons, and then it had seized them. He'd lashed out instinctively and fallen from its grip, plummeting for what had seemed a great distance—a lethal distance, had he been a common sprite. As it was, he was merely covered in bruises and sporting a sprained wrist. He had no memory from the moment he'd landed but assumed the bird had swooped down to collect him.

"Oberon?! Oberon!"

He turned to see Puck's head poking out of a mound of twigs. He was a mess, scratched and bruised all over, but what drew Oberon's concern was the gash that stretched right across his torso. Bloody streaks were running down his stomach.

"You're all right," his servant said, smiling weakly as Oberon clambered over to his side. "You fell such a long way, I thought..."

"Don't be stupid," Oberon said briskly, inspecting the cut. It was shallow, which was a mercy, given it had been some time since the fairy king had last been called upon to remember any of his healing magic.

Puck stroked his hair as he slowly cleaned and sealed up the wound. Only when it was closed, nothing left but a faint pink scar to remember it by, did Oberon realise how fiercely his heart was pounding.

"Oberon." Puck's slender hand came to rest upon his chest.

"Why didn't I see it coming? I've hunted in these woods for centuries. I've never been taken by surprise by an animal before," Oberon said, still staring at the pink scar marring Puck's body. To see any member of his mighty court wounded made his blood boil. To see his own servant thus, and knowing he'd sustained the injury in Oberon's presence, caused him as much shame as anger.

Puck clambered into his lap and set about nuzzling his neck. "Come on. We've both been in worse shape. Persephone's pips, you've *done* worse to me than this."

It was a joke, a tease to lighten the mood, but Oberon cringed all the same. Fairies had a reputation for being among the most casually violent of all the immortal species, and any love affair that didn't result in an occasional mutual mauling was considered an oddity. Even so, the memory of his brutality in the early days of their courtship was not one Oberon cherished. His role as a peevish lover had, more than once, become entangled with his role as a stern lord vexed by an oft-wayward underling. Despite Puck's extraordinary resilience to pain, Oberon often thought that if he had been in Puck's place, he would not have tolerated such misuse half so well.

He drew in a shuddering breath and took hold of himself. "Do you have any other injuries?"

"A bruise here, a scratch there, nothing that will slow me down. As to your earlier question, master, I think the reason you failed to spot the eagle before it attacked was because it was no ordinary beast on the hunt. I sensed some kind of spell on it, one designed to make it harder to see."

Oberon gritted his teeth, welcoming the flood of fury. "An assassination attempt?"

"I'd have thought so. But then why would the assassin not simply tell the beast to kill us? Why have us brought here?"

Before Oberon could respond, a voice he'd not heard in a long time said, "Good questions, all. I'm glad you've finally managed to find an advisor with a brain in his head."

Perched on the edge of the nest, towering over them both, was the eagle. Seated in a saddle affixed to the eagle's neck was a silver-haired fairy in her middle years.

"Queen Mab?" said Puck in bewilderment.

Oberon scowled. "Hello, Mother."

Chapter Two

I suppose it's easy to see where Oberon gets his looks from, Puck thought. *And his terrible manners.*

Mab leapt down from her mount, her wide, gold-tipped wings fanning out behind her like the fins of an elaborate goldfish. She had a stocky build and darker skin but was otherwise the mirror image of her son, right down to the sullen moue that appeared when Oberon didn't stand to greet her.

Puck would have done so—he didn't like to make enemies out of people he didn't know—had Oberon not had such a tight grip on him.

Oh, my love, Puck thought, fondly. *Of the two of us, she'd find me the more challenging opponent by far.*

"And he's pretty," Mab noted, still scrutinizing Puck. "Prettier than Titania, even. I'm sure she's terribly happy about that."

The eagle remained still, but Puck felt certain its gaze was fixed upon him. He shrunk back against Oberon's chest, eyes wide. He didn't object to most birds of prey, provided they remained a good distance away from him (Oberon's pet falcon and he had established a grudging respect based on the understanding Puck would not try to pull out its tail feathers if the falcon did not try to bite off his head). But eagles were such pitiless creatures, and this one had already had its claws in him.

"What do you want, Mother?" Oberon barked.

"Many things. A civil greeting. A son who writes. Grandchildren. But for the moment, I will content myself with a few minutes of your time."

She sat down cross-legged in front of them. Oberon assumed the same pose, still not releasing his grip on Puck. Wanting to be able to keep an eye on both Mab and the eagle, Puck wriggled until Oberon's chest was at his back and he was facing them.

"If you wanted to talk, you could have sent a letter. Or arranged a visit to my court. Or done any number of things that didn't involve sending your pet to attack me," said Oberon.

Mab shrugged. "If I had sent you a letter, you'd have ignored it. If I'd presented myself to your court, you'd have devised a million cunning excuses to avoid interacting with me. This seemed the surest way of getting your attention."

"She has a point, master," Puck said.

"Shush," Oberon said, his breath warm in Puck's ear. Obediently—for while he would provoke his master and flout his will in private, Puck would never deliberately embarrass him in company—Puck fell silent.

To his mother, Oberon said, "Well, you certainly have my attention now. Not only have you ruined my morning, you've scarred my favourite servant. Hellfire and damnation, woman, I've half a mind to exile you!"

"Half? I'd say a good two thirds of your mind is currently lodging in your manhood. Copulating in broad daylight, without any weapons at hand? I didn't raise you to be that stupid. And your servant's scar is an improvement. He possesses the sort of beauty that looks all the better for a little wear and tear."

"Thank you, my lady," Puck said sweetly, fluttering his eyelashes.

Wearily, Oberon repeated, "What do you *want*, Mother?"

"I've a message for you. From your father."

Oberon's face did not flicker, but this close, Puck could feel his heart speeding up. Confused, for he knew very little of Oberon's father, he placed a hand on Oberon's thigh to comfort him.

"And what does he want now?" Oberon rumbled.

"Don't take that tone with me," Mab snapped, and her eagle screeched in agreement. "I've spent years acting as your go-between, and a thankless duty it's been. Your father no longer speaks to me unless he has a message he wants me to take to you. I know you both hold me in contempt because I refuse to pick sides, but I'm still your mother, and you will address me with *respect*."

Oberon bowed his head sullenly, and she continued, "Your father says that he wants to reconcile."

Oberon's eyebrows are magnificent when they arch, Puck thought. *Like silver-coated stoats.*

"And you *believe* him?"

"Of course not. He wants something out of you, but I can't work out what it is. Here's the part you'll be interested in; he's made a peace offering."

"Ah. And what is it this time, I wonder? Diamonds? A magic sword? The moon on a golden string?"

Mab rolled her eyes heavenward. "Of all the traits I wish you had not inherited, my son, sarcasm is foremost. Your father says if you go visit him today, he will give you your wings back."

☆☆☆

"Master, is this wise?" Puck asked, half an hour later.

He flew alongside the eagle, which Mab had gifted to her son before departing. Oberon still hadn't fully worked out how to use the reins, and every now and then, his mount would veer sharply to one side, almost tipping him off, before returning to its course.

"Not wise. Necessary," Oberon replied, his voice muffled. He lay flat against the eagle's neck, enduring a mouthful of feathers for the decrease in wind resistance.

"Should we not at least arrive at your father's lair armed? We might well be walking into a trap."

"There would be no point in bringing weapons."

Puck brightened. "You are so confident in your skill?"

"No. My father's body and his magics are both far stronger than mine, and he can wield any weapon you care to name with far greater proficiency. He would interpret my arriving armed as a challenge."

They covered half a mile in silence as Puck chewed this over.

Quite suddenly, he went into a dive, disappearing into the trees below. Only mildly alarmed—for his servant's tendency towards sudden inexplicable actions had hardened his nerves—Oberon wondered if he should follow, only for Puck to emerge and rejoin him a moment later. He was now carrying an armful of leaves and flowers.

"If he's as bad as you say, I think it's best to make a good first impression," Puck told him. Landing on the eagle's back, he set about fashioning them both some new clothes.

They flew west for a further two hours. Puck could have devised a spell to let them cover the distance in far less time, but neither knew what awaited them, and Oberon thought it wise that he conserve his magic. Finally, just as the heat of the day was becoming unbearable, a tall shadow appeared on the horizon.

"By all the gods! What is it?" Puck gasped. "A giant?"

"No. My father's court."

It was the tallest tree in the region, quite possibly one of the tallest in the world. Oberon's father had procured its seed from foreign shores millennia ago and aided its growth with magic, and now it protruded from the canopy and loomed over its neighbours like a dire wolf in a world of lapdogs. Its upper third was an impenetrable mass of branches and leaves, and Oberon remembered that long ago, as a boy, he'd entertained himself by hiding amongst them. A jolly game, until he'd realised the reason no one ever found him was because no one ever looked, or even noticed his absence.

It was quiet as they drew near, and Puck pressed against his back. His nearness made Oberon recall their interrupted love play, and he silently cursed his father once again.

"Let's not let him see us coming," his canny servant told him. "Why don't we set the eagle down there and walk the rest of the way?"

Acknowledging the wisdom in this, Oberon spent several minutes trying to work out how to land his new pet. Eventually, when he'd managed to coerce it down to a height of just a few metres above the ground, the eagle lost its patience and simply shook them both off.

"Nasty beast!" Puck admonished it, catching Oberon and bringing them both gently down to the forest floor.

Before they approached the tree, he insisted on tending to Oberon's apparel and putting the finishing touches on his own new clothes, which included a leaf cape and a jaunty hat of pansy petals.

"Master," he said as he fashioned Oberon's hair into a complicated asymmetrical braid, of the sort he wore on diplomatic excursions. "What is your father's nature?"

"Clever. Selfish. Perceptive. A competent politician," said Oberon. "And he enjoys games."

Puck clapped his hands. "Ah! A commonality of interest! Does he play mouse polo?"

"Not those sorts of games."

"Oh."

Then, tentatively, Puck said, "Before we get there, are you going to tell me what happened? Why he...did what he did to you?"

"I already told you. We had an argument, he tore off my wings, we haven't spoken since."

"Ah. I see. My master doesn't love me enough to tell me all his secrets." Puck sniffed. "I suppose I shouldn't let it upset me. I am, after all, but a servant. It's just that I had come to believe I had earned my way into his majesty's trust...that I was more to him than a mere bed-warmer and errand boy...but I see now how misguided I was. Forgive my hubris, master."

Oberon regarded his trembling lower lip sourly. "You are a conniving fiend."

Puck nodded.

"It's a very dull story," Oberon said. "When I was on the cusp on manhood, he chose a bride for me. I told him I had no interest in marrying someone I'd never met. The ensuing quarrel was extremely bitter. Shortly afterwards, my father caught me with my first lover, who was a guard.

"He was angry; although to this day, I'm not sure whether his anger stemmed from the fact that my lover was a man, or he was beneath my station, or I was flaunting my father's authority. We fought; he won. He took my wings off and exiled me from his court. Titania's family were friends of my mother; they took me in, on the condition that I marry their daughter when we both came of age. Given that my only alternative was surrendering all hope of ever attaining real power again and accepting a life of obscurity, I agreed."

The clipped, inflectionless voice he used wasn't an attempt to cover up a deep well of inner grief. He had never particularly liked his father, and while he was still *angry*, he'd long since made peace with his lot. Becoming co-ruler of the most powerful fairy kingdom in the world did quite a bit to soothe one's grievances.

No, the voice was more for Puck's sake. Oberon had told his story to only five or six people in all the centuries since it had happened. In every case, their reaction had revealed a facet of themselves with which he had not previously been familiar. Those who prided themselves on being good souls tended to get a certain unsettling light in their eyes even as syrupy platitudes dribbled over their lips. Such people, he had found, were drawn to the misfortunes of others like maggots to a corpse and derived perverse gratification from extending pity to those who did not need it.

Oh, you poor man.

It's natural to grieve.

Remember that such challenges only make us stronger.

Perhaps it was for the best. You never know.

His Puck was host to no such signs of low character. But he might take it into his mercurial mind that Oberon would like his father's skin as an anniversary present. And while Oberon was confident in Puck's ability to survive a battle with his sire, he did not feel the same confidence for the fate of everything within a hundred mile radius of such a battle.

"Is your first lover still here?" Puck asked, his wings flicking jealously.

"I've no idea. I've heard no news of him in years. It is possible that my father decided to dismiss him after exiling me."

"Was he better-looking than me?"

Oberon shrugged, staring deliberately at Puck's groin. "Parts of him were."

With a shriek, his servant fell upon him like a wildcat. Oberon allowed himself to be pushed over onto the grass, and Puck balanced on his chest with his hands at his throat.

"I will make you forget he and his *parts* ever existed, Oberon," he hissed.

He set about deftly removing his king's new attire, his nimble fingers prodding sharply at Oberon's person. Amused, Oberon lay back and reflected upon his servant's features; his heart-shaped face and pointy chin, his olive skin, and his lips—the exact same pale pink as the inside of a sea shell he'd gifted Oberon last time they'd visited the shoreline.

There had been a period of his life when Oberon had associated such beauty as indicative of falseness when it manifested in men. That was why, when he had first encountered Puck, he'd assumed the sprite was not only shrewd and sharp-tongued, but likely underhanded as well. The assumption was, in fact, one of the main reasons he'd invited him to join his court; underhanded advisors were usually the best kind. But he'd long since realised his mistake. For all his guile, Puck was instinctively inclined towards honesty and was, in many ways, oddly innocent.

This was most plainly apparent in his unguarded reactions in intimate moments. When at last Puck had Oberon's cock before him, just beginning to swell, he stopped and gazed at it for a moment with something like wonder. He did that quite often, and it always gave Oberon a fluttery feeling in his chest, a combination of fondness and smugness.

The fairy king knew himself to be handsome enough, but his cock was the only part of his body he took a somewhat childish pride in. It was thick, even for one of his size and stature, and seemed to him to have a particularly pleasing curve. In the years before Puck, when all he had for comfort was a compulsory annual coupling with his wife and the occasional solicitation of an underling hoping to win his favour, he'd pleasured himself whenever there was enough time and privacy to do so. He'd never needed a fantasy. The sight of his hand moving up and down his erection had been enough by itself.

Puck caressed his shaft and then applied his tongue to the tip without artistry, but with more than enough enthusiasm to make up for it.

"One of the things I remember most about my first lover is his flexibility. He could suck his own cock," Oberon said, because sex was always more fun when one of them was feeling murderously covetous.

Puck's muted growl made his balls tighten. Suddenly greedy, Oberon reached down and pulled him off, ignoring his protests in favour of turning him over and roughly forcing him down onto the grass.

"Er...here, master?" said Puck as Oberon clambered on top of him. "I don't have any oil with me."

"Shut up and keep your legs together," Oberon breathed, placing a palm over his servant's heart and feeling it race. The next quiver of Puck's wings showered them both in fairy dust.

It wasn't quite the incomparable perfection of fucking his servant's arse. But that took time, and yes, a lot of oil, neither of which they had to spare at the moment. And Puck's thighs were a wholly satisfactory substitute, smooth and slender and strong as they were, and moreover, Oberon found the position itself very pleasing. Looming over the smaller fairy's body, watching him arch and perspire from above, gave him the giddy exhilaration of a fox with a rabbit's throat in its jaws.

"Mine," he growled.

Puck shot him a grin and clenched his thighs tightly together. Another two hard thrusts and Oberon came, biting on Puck's pointed ear as though he meant to tear it off. As soon as he regained muscle coordination, he dragged Puck's hips off the ground and took hold of his cock.

"By the gods, I've been waiting for this all day," Puck sighed as Oberon began to work him to completion.

And then a new voice interjected, "And I have been waiting for *you* all day, my wayward son."

Chapter Three

Puck swore an oath as Oberon's hand stopped moving.

"I warn you, interloper, I am far less merry and bright when sexually frustrated," he snarled, turning his head in the direction of the voice. "I suggest you...oh."

"Well met, Father," Oberon said curtly, rolling off Puck's back and snatching up their garments.

Puck, who had never felt the slightest bit ashamed of his body, clothed or unclothed, took his time donning his leaves and pansy hat, more interested in drinking in the sight of Oberon's sire. Although rumour and hearsay suggested that Lord Ariel must have been at least ten thousand years old, his face was as smooth as a looking glass. He looked very little like Oberon; his features were narrower, more delicate, and his skin was moon pale. His hair was a tumbling mass of copper curls, and he adorned himself in a tunic of dandelion petals. At the moment, he stood in a patch of sunlight, an ornate staff in one hand, and regarded them both with boredom.

"Hello, Oberon," he said, in a light and musical voice. "Still molesting the help, I see."

Oh goodness, I do not think we will get on, thought Puck, longing for his whip.

Oberon was already bristling. Nonetheless, he performed the traditional half bow that implied respect and goodwill between fairy rulers and said in a controlled voice, "Father, this is my first advisor and beloved, Robin Goodfellow. An insult to him is an insult to me."

It was the first time Oberon had introduced him as anything other than "my servant," and while Puck was charmed, he was also mortified to hear him give out his real name. Thankfully, the embarrassment helped to wilt his still-rather-prominent erection.

"Yes, I've heard of him," Ariel said, returning the bow. He cast an eye over Puck in a manner reminiscent of a someone trying to decide whether or not to purchase an ageing halibut for dinner. "What a dreadful hat. Is he entirely bereft of taste?"

Clever, thought Puck. Oberon could rein in his temper where insults directed towards himself were concerned, but slighting his allies was the fastest possible way of cutting the reins.

"I didn't come here to trade barbs with you, Ariel," Oberon snapped. "Where are my wings? And what do you want in exchange?"

At the first sign of his son's anger, Ariel's expression thawed into a warm smile. His voice became almost playful. "Still the same impatient Oberon. It's good to know some things never change. Although some certainly do—look how tall you've gotten! Almost a proper adult now. Come on, then."

He turned and took to the air, flying off in the direction of the tree. Puck couldn't help but notice that Lord Ariel's wings were things of wonder, similar in shape to those of a dragonfly and pale blue with shimmering silver edges.

"Sprite, whichever part of my sire you are currently dragging your eyes over, may I kindly request that you desist?" grumbled Oberon.

Puck took his hand and kissed his palm in apology. "Forgive me, master. I was merely observing that Lord Ariel's wings are not without appeal, and that, should he refuse to surrender to you what is yours, perhaps I might procure them for you."

Chastened, Oberon stroked his cheek, and they both moved to follow Ariel.

☆☆☆

Like any powerful fairy court, Ariel's saw its share of travelling merchants, performers, and diplomats, many of whom were elves or goblins. To accommodate such wingless guests, a spiralling staircase had been carved into the tree's mighty trunk. As Oberon ascended, Puck following three paces behind him as was proper, they passed by dozens, if not hundreds of cavities, such as a mortal might think were occupied by squirrels. He peered into many, but only now and then did he catch sight of an occupant peering back. His father's court had shrunk since his departure.

The staircase eventually stopped just as the tree began putting out its branches, and they proceeded by climbing from one to the next. When they were deeply immersed in the foliage, it was as dark as twilight. Ariel awaited them on a slender bough.

"By the way, how is your queen these days?" he asked as Oberon drew level with him. "Still no children, I take it?"

"I refer you to my earlier point about barbs and the trading thereof. Where are my wings?"

Ariel shook his head. "Still no children. I don't understand it. Neither does your mother. We did very well in the making of you. Whatever your internal flaws, outwardly you are sheer perfection. It seems foolish, even malicious, for one as privileged as you to lead your graces to the grave and leave the world no copy."

"My wings. Where are they?"

"Your mother once speculated there may be some sort of...problem." Ariel glanced at Oberon's groin before resuming. "I told her the idea was absurd. Men of our line have never had any difficulty begetting children. Mind you, men of our line also didn't make a habit of seducing their social inferiors."

The dim twilight amidst the tree's branches became dimmer still as a shadow moved over the sun. The temperature dropped sharply, and from somewhere far in the distance, there came a crack of thunder.

"*Such* impatience," Ariel sighed. "Very well. I have decided to give you back your wings, Oberon, *if* you prove yourself worthy."

"I see. Another of your games, then. How will my worth be measured this time? Shall I wrestle a bear? Or count the number of termites within a thousand mile radius?"

"Sarcasm is unbecoming. All you have to do is find them."

"A treasure hunt, then. How quaint. And the parameters?"

Ariel spread his arms. "That's the best part! I've hidden them somewhere on the tree. Enchanted so as to look like leaves. But they will reveal themselves to you when you get close enough."

Staring at the mass of foliage surrounding them, Puck said, "But that is a terrible game! What quality does it measure? Not courage, not wit, not honour. Only blind luck."

"Luck...and persistence," said Ariel. "Both of which I consider to be essential qualities in anyone who considers themselves worthy to wear a crown. And even if you have no luck, the game is winnable. If you look long enough, you *will* find them, eventually."

"Very well, Father. Puck, we will begin—"

Quickly, Ariel said, "No. I'm afraid that would make the game much too easy. Your servant is known to be a skilled magician. Moreover, I have heard it said that his wings are so powerful he can girdle the earth in forty minutes. An exaggeration, I'm sure, but even so, I must insist he wait here with me while you search alone."

Puck opened his mouth to protest, before Oberon cut him off. "There's no point arguing with him. Remain here; I will not be long. And don't eat anything he offers you."

So saying, he ascended to the next branch and began to inspect its leaves. Then he climbed onto the next one, and the next, and the next, until Puck and his father were out of sight.

☆☆☆

As soon as Oberon had disappeared from view, lost in the density of leaves, Ariel clapped his hands and turned to Puck. "*Finally.* I was beginning to think I'd never get him out of the way. Now we can have a proper talk."

The lordly snobbery that had saturated his tone just moments ago vanished once again. Wrong-footed, Puck replied, "You wish to speak to me, Lord Ariel? Could you not have done so in my master's presence?"

Ariel waved a hand. "No, no, it's impossible to discuss anything frankly when he's about. He's so temperamental. So difficult to reason with."

"Then this game of yours was devised solely for the purpose of diverting his attention? It seems to me that you could have simply sent him to retrieve his wings from an accessible cupboard. Or else written me a letter, sparing us both the deception."

His blue eyes glittering with mischief, Ariel said, "Oh, that was just a spot of fun. I used to make up all sorts of sports and puzzles for him when he was small. Once, I devised a cunning box, with a lock that could only be opened when you solved a riddle. Then for the next week, I would hide his meals in it, so he could only eat once he'd worked out the answer. Hah! He'd throw the most outrageous tantrums you ever did see. He's so terribly funny when he's cross."

A trace of nostalgia had entered his voice.

Puck had never found Oberon's anger amusing. Frightening, and sometimes beautiful in the way of a tropical storm, but never amusing. But what an effective tactic that was. *He's so terribly funny when he's cross.* When the abused rebelled, how easily, how casually the abuser's mirth could strip away all the power of their anger. Puck himself, in dark days he did not care to remember, had once dwelled amongst people who had found it *charming* and *dear* and *cute* when he became enraged or upset.

I'm going to kill you, Puck realised suddenly, the notion so strong it felt like foretelling. *I really am. Maybe not today, but one day.*

The knowledge was an anchor in his soul and allowed him to maintain his composure. He laughed gaily and said, "A merry jest indeed, my lord! But what did you want to discuss?"

Ariel's wings, Puck noticed, glowed as he spoke, becoming brighter when he emphasised his words and dimmer when he lowered his voice. For fairies, this was the equivalent of a peacock spreading its tail feathers before a likely mate, and Puck thought,

Euuurgh. No.

"Firstly, I wanted to offer my congratulations. I'd heard of you and your exploits long before you became part of my son's court, but even so, I never expected you to work your way into his graces as quickly as you did, nor as thoroughly. I know that boy like the back of my hand. He's not simply lusting after you; he's infatuated with you. And by all accounts, you've served him well. The relationship between his court and its neighbours has improved dramatically; more and more of his fairies are learning to write and to read as mortals do, and their hunts are yielding fewer and fewer casualties every season. All thanks to your guidance and magics, or so I'm told."

"Lies and embellishments, my lord. King Oberon and Queen Titania are both supremely competent rulers in their own right. Many of the improvements are the result of their wise planning and labour."

"Yes, yes, I'm sure you're careful to disown responsibility. I imagine it suits your purposes to pass yourself off as nothing but the king's flighty concubine. But I know my son. Oberon is not entirely without intelligence, but he's bereft of self-control, and worse, he's a brooder. Such men are not made to lead. As for Queen Titania...well, she may well be a savvy politician, but let's be frank, Puck. No one really *likes* her, do they? With that long mule's face of hers, and her strident voice, she'll never be the sort of monarch her subjects could fall in love with. They may respect her, but you know what our people are like. We need to love those who lead us."

Puck nodded sagely, only half listening. He was preoccupied in developing a fantasy in which he removed Ariel's teeth and toenails and swapped them around, prior to setting Oberon's new pet on him.

Ariel continued, "You, Robin Goodfellow, are very good at making yourself lovable, aren't you? It is an invaluable skill. It is a skill my court needs."

His fantasy dispersing, Puck sputtered, "You...you're offering me a *job*?"

"Your salary would be substantial. My court is not so grand as my son's, but it is far richer. And I would give you a proper title. No more of this 'my advisor and beloved' nonsense. 'Chancellor Robin'. How does that sound?"

Unable to help himself, Puck placed his fingers across his mouth and chortled. "You are repulsive and inane. But thank you, thank you very much. When my master has found his wings, we will have a merry time laughing at you. Good grief. You disturbed my holiday for this?"

The mischievous twinkle disappeared, and the aristocratic chill settled back into place.

"You've heard the story of how my son lost his wings?" Ariel asked.

"Is that a threat, my lord?" Puck asked, inspecting his nails and thinking, *I do hope it is.*

"No. I am attempting to assess how intimate your relationship with Oberon is."

"Very. He told me everything. You caught him in a tryst with some silly admirer and lost your temper."

"Ah. And you took his word for it. Funny, they told me you were clever. No, what actually happened was that I caught him bedding a commoner who my son then insisted was his 'beloved.' Oberon declared to my face that he'd never adored anyone as much, and never would again, and then threatened to publicly surrender his crown if I tried to keep them apart. It was quite touching.

"The point is I didn't cut off his wings because I was angry. It was done—with much regret—in the hopes of preventing them from eloping. It didn't work; Oberon continued to defy my will and made plans to leave. But then his lover informed him he didn't particularly *want* to elope with him. Terribly awkward business, you can imagine. My son made a positively disgraceful show of grief. By that point, I was so sick of the whole business I exiled him just to restore some semblance of order to my court. I expected him to come crawling back in a few months, repentant, whereupon I would happily have returned his wings to him. But he never came back. Too proud. He did, however, maintain regular correspondence with his erstwhile beloved, even throughout his engagement to Titania."

Puck digested this slowly. "I think you're trying to make me jealous."

"I am. And it's working, isn't it?"

It was. Alarmingly well. Puck had always disliked knowing he had not been Oberon's first, as Oberon had been his, but he had contented himself with the belief he was the first Oberon had ever truly worshiped.

"Good day, my lord," he said abruptly and flew off before he could succumb to violence.

Chapter Four

He flew in loops about the forest, burning away his irritation. Ariel, he reminded himself again and again, was not to be trusted. And what did it matter if Oberon had been in love before?

But, oh, *oh*, how he simmered at the thought of some tall, rakishly handsome guard seducing his master years before Puck had even laid eyes on him. How *dare* he? How had he accomplished it? Surely, even in his youth, Oberon would have been too introspective to fall for a pretty face and a few beguiling words? No, no. Far more likely that Ariel's dubious methods of parenting had left Puck's master starved for love, and he'd latched himself onto the nearest source of affection. Yes, that was it. The wretched seducer had preyed upon the vulnerable prince, and then, when he was finished with him, he'd cast him aside. How *dare* he?

And worst of all, to think Oberon had been so desperately in love that he'd been on the verge of surrendering his crown, his princely status. Oberon *loved* ruling, was born to rule, would not be Oberon if he were not royalty. He had remained in a loveless marriage all these years purely because to pursue divorce would likely end in his losing his place as king. Certainly, Puck could not imagine that Oberon would ever surrender his crown for *his* sake...

Puck shook such evil thoughts off and made another loop before heading back to the tree. By the time he finally found Oberon, his mood was utterly rotten.

"Never, not in a thousand years, will you believe what your father just said to me," he huffed as he dropped down to the branch upon which the fairy king was carefully inspecting a new cluster of leaves.

"Since your entrance into my life, my capacity for disbelief has been beaten into submission," Oberon muttered, absorbed in his search. "Go away. You're not supposed to be helping me."

"I'm not helping you; I'm airing my grievances. Your father just insulted both you and the queen to my face, and then he asked me to be his chancellor. Can you believe the nerve?"

Oberon shrugged, still not looking his way. "He's always liked to get his hands on my things. Often in the past, when I've dismissed someone from my service for some or other misdemeanour, he's snatched them up and made them his."

"Aren't you outraged?" Puck asked, coming to hang off his arm. "He tried to *buy* me, like a mare in a mortal marketplace. It was infuriating."

Oberon shook him off with a grunt. "Outrage can wait. I still have roughly one million leaves to examine and no desire to spend a second longer in my father's court than necessary. Ignore him. Whatever you do, don't provoke his ire. And now leave me in peace."

Puck flew off in a huff for the second time that day.

Hours later, he sat nestled amongst the thorns of a wild rose bush, not far from Ariel's tree. It seemed a good place for brooding, which was just as well. As he watched the sun set, silhouetting the tree against a golden sky, Puck descended into a most melancholy humour.

As was often the case, he sought a way to let the world know about it, for Puck did not believe in suffering in silence when there might be others about whom he could make just as miserable as he. But his closest companions were a family of squirrels and a mole snake slithering through the undergrowth. It occurred to him that he might distract himself from his woes by murdering one or the other for his dinner, but unhappiness tended to reduce his appetite, and moreover, he had no bow. So instead, he elected to recite some poetry to them.

Throwing back his head and conjuring up the most dramatically mournful tone imaginable, he sang,

"You draw me, you hard-hearted adamant;

But yet you draw not iron, for my heart
Is true as steel: leave you your power to draw…"

"And I shall have no power to follow you," came another voice.

Oberon! Puck thought, delighted, and turned to greet his master. But to his disappointment, Oberon was nowhere to be seen. Instead, standing at the foot of the rose bush, there was a short, plain-faced fairy with a round belly and pudgy legs gazing up at him curiously. His wings were red-brown, and his hair was tied up in a messy bun.

Puck was truly puzzled. The lines he had recited belonged to sweet William's silly play. How had this unknown creature learned them?

"Did I get it right?" the fairy asked him. "It is 'no power', isn't it? Or is it 'no will'?"

Jumping down, Puck said, "You got it right, stranger. But how do you know it?"

"Oh, I love poetry," he said, looking bashful. He wore a mousehide tunic, and on his back, there was a short spear, functional but unattractive. "It's a hobby. I used to favour the old goblin epics, but in the last few centuries, the mortals have produced some extraordinary work—John Gower's been my favourite for a while, but the modern playwrights are winning me over. They're so vibrant, so good at clever double-meanings. But it sounds much better in your voice than mine. You say it just the way the actors do."

"I helped write it," Puck boasted. "The author is an old friend of mine."

"Truly?"

"Truly. What's your name?"

The fairy straightened up and executed a well-rehearsed bow, if lacking in elegance. "Bunce, third-in-command of Lord Ariel's guardsmen, pleased to meet you. I'm out on patrol; we sometimes get wolves around these parts. I say, you're Puck, aren't you? I've heard of your legs."

Pleased, Puck extended one into the last ray of sunlight, showing off his spiralling tattoos. "They are rather fine, aren't they?"

"If you're here, then King Oberon must be as well," said Bunce, his voice becoming momentarily subdued. "You haven't left him alone with Ariel, have you? They used to have the most dreadful fights."

"They are not talking at present. And my absence from the king's side is not by choice. He has important business to attend to." *Important, farcical business.*

"Good Puck, may I ask why you were reciting those particular lines? Helena's such a sad character; I always feel sorry for her. Are you also in love with someone out of your reach?"

"Helena's not sad; she's absurd," Puck retorted. "I'd barely even call her a character. She's a prop. A tottering tower of needy nothingness. None of the humans in that play are much good, but she's the worst of them. It's just that her lines are particularly suited to those moments when one wants to indulge in self-pity."

"I think that's a bit cruel," Bunce ventured. "But I suppose that might be because I see myself in her. I've had my share of hopeless loves."

Happy to have found an amiable companion and keen for a juicy story or two to repair his mood, Puck sat back on a plump blue rose. "Tell me more. I have nothing with which to occupy myself for the next few hours—unless you would prefer we recite more poetry to each other?"

Bunce laughed and fluttered up to sit alongside him. "No, no, you'd be loathe to see my Lysander. All right, let's swap our stories. Here's something most people don't know about me; for a brief period in my youth, I had a lover who was of noble birth."

"Oooh. They're always fun. What was their name?"

Placing a hand beside his mouth, Bunce said in a stage whisper, "*Oberon* himself."

☆☆☆

What was known among immortals as "fairy wine" was made

from plums and algae and laced with spells that served to make it bubble it your mouth. It took an expert two years to make, most of which was spent waiting for the spells to rot thoroughly enough to render it safe to drink. Putting magic in comestibles was a risky business.

But when all you wanted was to get drunk as quickly as possible, there was always nectar. And that, thank the gods, required no preparation at all.

"I am sorry," Bunce said as Puck stuck his head in another bluebell.

After slurping up as much as he could in one go, Puck emerged. His eyes felt red and swollen, and there was pollen clinging to his nose. "No, no, it's not your fault. I'm sorry for shouting. And for calling you fat. Although you are. 'Flexible,' indeed."

His manners always fell by the wayside when he was inebriated.

"I was fat then, too," said Bunce with dignity. "He seemed to like it."

"Aargh," said Puck, sticking his head back into the bloom.

Speaking into it, Bunce said, "It didn't last very long. I always knew it wouldn't. He was a prince, and...well, I was infatuated with him, but I never really imagined spending the rest of our lives together. Apart from anything else, I like my job, and I didn't want Ariel to exile me to the far north. But you know how Oberon is once he gets an idea into his head. He decided he was in love with me, and he made this awfully dramatic speech to his father, while I was standing right there like a ninny. It was touching, but also very embarrassing. I never expected Ariel to do what he did."

Withdrawing his head a second time, Puck slurred, "You *didn't*? I barely know the man, and even I can tell he's a serpent."

"He wasn't always like that. Anyway, then Oberon invited me to run away with him, and I said no. I didn't enjoy hurting him, but as I said, I didn't want to lose my job."

"So you let my poor master go off into the world maimed and disinherited and all alone," Puck said venomously. Then he sniffed and added, "*I* would sacrifice a thousand jobs for Oberon's sake."

"I don't doubt it, but then it's different for you. You're clever and good-looking and you know magic and you like moving about. You can do anything you want. You could get a post in any fairy court in the world. Me, I'm good at one thing, and that's being a guard. Running off with Oberon would have been lovely, for a while, but where would I ever have found employment when it was known throughout the land that I'd betrayed Lord Ariel's trust?"

Wiping the pollen off his nose, Puck gazed at Ariel's tree. It was a beauty at night, its trunk speckled with fairy lights and soft green glows coming from deep within its branches.

"You speak wisely," he said and jumped into the air. "I believe I shall go shout at my master."

"Is there *anything* I can do to help?" Bunce asked.

"You can find where that blasted eagle's gone. We may need to make a hasty getaway."

Being half drunk made navigating his way through the branches of Ariel's tree even more difficult. He came dangerously close to an owl, who he assumed must be one of Ariel's pets, else it wouldn't have been permitted so near to his court. He finally found Oberon not far from where he had last left him, in much the same pose, examining a cluster of leaves that seemed identical to every other cluster of leaves.

"I'm here to help," Puck announced and hiccoughed.

Oberon glared at him. He looked exhausted. "You heard my father. You're not allowed."

"I don't give a fig for your father's stupid game and his stupid rules. He doesn't need to know. I'll help you look, and as soon as we've found them, we'll both make a run for it before he can stop us."

The glare intensified. "I do not need to run from Ariel, sprite."

"But master, you already did so once. Why is it different now?"

"I did not *run!*" Oberon snarled. "I was exiled. I didn't flee like a thief in the night. We will play my father's game, I will *win*, and then we will leave."

One of the reasons most fairies preferred wine to nectar was because of the speed with which hangovers set in. Puck rubbed his head. "Master, consider this. Many creatures are born without wings—goblins, nymphs, humans, lions, spiders. And some fairies, too. Most of them don't seem to notice the lack. They consider their bodies perfectly whole—different, not lesser."

"You imply I am being unreasonable in working to undo my maiming?"

"No, no, I...all I mean, master, is that being without wings is a state of being to which many excellent people are accustomed. I am certain I would not find you any more magnificent than you already are, were you to regain your wings."

It was the truth, and it was what Puck would have wanted said to him, but it didn't seem to help matters.

"Your opinion is noted," Oberon said coldly. "Now leave."

Puck's wings began to twitch with restrained anger. To be rudely dismissed by his king *twice* in one day?

"Apropos your disinclination to demean your honour by fleeing, my liege," he said through gritted teeth, "it might be observed that you have never been so concerned for what others might think of you in the past. Your entire court knows you only share Queen Titania's bed to fulfil an obligation."

"Watch your words," Oberon growled.

But once Puck had let his tongue loose, it was difficult to rein it back in. "You've never seemed troubled by the impact of that knowledge on your reputation, oh great one. By the fact that there are some members of your court who speak of how Oberon 'prostitutes himself for his crown', and—"

With a roar, Oberon struck Puck's face, throwing him off the branch upon which they were standing and into the one adjacent. Addled, Puck fell several feet before catching himself. As he did, his tongue detected a strange abscess in the left side of his mouth, and he realised Oberon's blow had dislodged a tooth.

Enraged beyond reason, he shrieked, "Do you have *any idea* how long that will take me to fix? Do you think conjuring up new teeth is *easy*, you *fucking cur*?!"

He snapped his fingers, and all the night-time bugs and insects that had been buzzing nearby came together in a great black swarm and dove straight for Oberon's face. Puck did not stay to cheer them on, but instead flew downwards to seek out his tooth.

It was while he was on his hands and knees peering into the grass at the bottom of the tree, struggling to see clearly in the moonlight, that Bunce caught up with him.

"Puck!" cried the guard. "I say, whatever happened to your face?"

"A fool and his temper," Puck hissed, running his fingers over the ground.

"I found your eagle; tied him up near the rose bush. Have you lost something?"

"A tooth. Be careful where you step."

"Did...did *Oberon* do that?"

"His royal highness is not fit for company at the moment. I presented a perfectly reasonable argument and received nothing but a sound clobbering for my efforts."

They scoured the ground together, but privately, Puck had all but given up hope of locating his tooth. He'd need to go all the way to the mortal realm to procure the proper ingredients for a potion that would allow him to grow a new one. Brewing it would take weeks of tedious measurements, and the potion itself was temperamental and often didn't work. *Damn* Oberon.

But then Bunce held up something small and white, and Puck squealed with joy as Bunce placed it into his hand.

"You shouldn't say it like that," Bunce told him. "'Clobbered' makes it sound silly, like a joke. It's not a joke. He shouldn't have done that to you."

Puck regarded Bunce's face and was surprised at the amount of genuine concern it showed. Touched, and somewhat puzzled, he leant over and pressed a kiss onto Bunce's cheek. "Of course not, but you needn't look so worried. I'm hardier than I look. Watch."

Brushing dirt off the tooth, he opened his mouth and spent a few moments wiggling it around until it was back in place. Then he waved his fingers, and his jaw tingled as the spell repaired nerve endings and gum tissue.

"Good as new," he said, showing off his restored smile.

Bunce didn't appear mollified. In fact, he seemed even more upset than he had been before, his wings drooping unhappily.

I'm sticking both feet in my mouth tonight, Puck thought.

"I'm sure you can take care of yourself, good Puck, but he's not going to stop if you just put up with it," the plump fairy said solemnly. "I know you're in love with him, but you're not going to...to change him. You do know that?"

"I don't want to change him," Puck replied indignantly. "Why would I want something I love to change? I don't love mussel stew because I expect it to metamorphose into cabbage soup halfway through my eating it."

"You shouldn't be glib. It's serious."

Puck sighed, feeling old. "You're kind, but you don't know us. You think he has some hold over me, that I'm deluded by my love for him. You're wrong. The fact is we're both violent people, he with his fists and I with my words. Of the two, I suspect I do the greater damage. This was a squabble, not a betrayal. Believe me, I am familiar with betrayal. Had he lied to me, or pried into my affairs, or attempted to constrain my wanderings—these things would have been a betrayal to me. But a blow? I don't mind a blow. Well, yes, I mind. But he's only hurt the outside of me. Do you understand?"

Bunce mulled this over. "Had my lover struck me, *I* would consider that a most rank betrayal."

"But you are not I. And truly, I wasn't jesting when I said I'm hardier than I look."

Fixing his eyes on the ground, Bunce mumbled, "I shouldn't tell you this, but...Lord Ariel approached me while you were gone. He wants me to persuade you to join his court. He was quite insistent."

"Dear me. The poor man must be desperate."

"To be honest with you, I think he's just bored. His son is gone, his wife only returns home once in a blue moon, and he considers the rest of us beneath him. He wants you in his service not just because of your renowned wit, but because you'd be someone to talk to."

"How sad," said Puck without sympathy. "Perhaps he should get a pet." Standing, he brushed the dirt off his knees. "Now, my lord isn't going to finish up any time soon, and I'm starving. Why don't you tell me where Ariel keeps his larder?"

Chapter Five

Hours later, the first rays of sunlight illuminated not a forest, but a sea of pale mist from which Ariel's mighty tree arose like a lighthouse. Breakfasting on a blackberry, Ariel admired the view and the picturesque vision his son made silhouetted against it, his chin in his hand, his strong back hunched. He felt a stab of jealousy. Oberon seemed able to project an aura of drama and magnificence effortlessly, even when at his lowest ebb. Ariel himself had to choreograph his public appearances to achieve such an effect.

"Well met," he greeted his son, blackberry juice running down his chin. "No luck? Still haven't found them? Never mind. You'll get there eventually. By the way, I couldn't help but observe the altercation you had with your servant last night."

Oberon replied, "So you have been spying on me. I wondered."

He didn't sound angry. *Curious.*

"Of course. And I confess myself staggered by the depths of his insolence. Had one of mine addressed me in such a fashion, I'd have cut out his heart. Your response was peculiarly mild."

"I struck him," Oberon said with an agonised wrench in his voice that confirmed several of Ariel's suspicions. "Without moderation."

"You did. And let me tell you, Oberon, it did my heart good. I'd begun to worry that he'd completely castrated you. You might not remember, but I often had to reprimand your mother in a similar fashion. I won't pretend one doesn't feel like a beast afterwards, but it's the only real way to keep them in line."

"Yes. I do remember you doing that."

Was that *reproach* he detected in his son's voice?

"I never struck *you*, though," Ariel reminded him. "Not once.

Don't I get a few points for that? Anyway, do cheer up. You're making fabulous progress. And your servant is keeping himself entertained. He's met up with your old favourite, the fat one."

Finally, anger. Oberon's eyes flashed red. "Don't refer to him in such a manner. Whatever crimes I may have committed against you, he's served you faithfully all his life."

Ariel was simply unable to resist replying, "He has. In so many ways."

And he licked his lips.

☆☆☆

As the mist slowly dispersed and the world freshened up, most of Ariel's court still had not returned home. They had been drawn from their tree in the wee hours, to a nearby glade where a lithe foreign fellow had made a bonfire and was telling the most marvellous stories and jokes.

None of them were to know that the fuel for Puck's bonfire consisted largely of objects he had stolen from Ariel's larder and treasury. Bunce, interestingly enough, had made only a token effort to stop him and now sat laughing and clapping with the others. Puck suspected Ariel's guardsman, while innately loyal, had begun to grow disillusioned with his master after so many years of service.

"Now," Puck said. "Who wants to hear the tale of the time I turned a mortal into a donkey?"

As several dozen hands went up, the day darkened. Confused, Puck observed that several pitch-black storm clouds had rolled over what had been, just minutes ago, a perfect blue sky. Several of those gathered around him cried out as thunder boomed and a great flash of lightning lit up the glade.

"Oh, drat," Puck murmured and leapt into the air. He flew straight upwards and rose above the canopy just in time to see lightning strike the top of Ariel's tree.

In the baking heat of the last few days, the tree's leaves had grown very dry, and from within its topmost branches there emerged a plume of smoke.

Puck dove towards it shouting Oberon's name, but he could barely hear the sound of his own voice over the thunder.

Girdle the earth in forty minutes. An exaggeration, but not much of one. He sped over and under the tree's branches, several of which were now on fire, at such speed he'd have been invisible to mortal eyes. Within seconds, he had found them, father and son, standing on a branch now flaming at both ends and doing their best to murder one another.

Puck slammed into them both like a comet into a custard pie and sent them flying. He didn't see where Ariel landed, if he did, but instead rushed to catch Oberon before he could plunge into the flames.

"Puck," said his master as he wrapped both arms around him. Oberon looked dreadful, his face bearing not only the cuts and bruises inflicted by Ariel, but also the stings of Puck's earlier insectile assault. He'd obviously inhaled a good deal of smoke and was babbling. "Forgive me. I am a fool. How could I ever enjoy my wings if I knew I'd earned them by performing tricks for my father like...like a circus pony? You were right to criticise me. You're always right, my Puck."

"This is true," Puck acknowledged, feeling both he and his ego were due a good stroking after yesterday's shenanigans. He flew until they were clear of the tree and the flames. "But I forgive you. And please forgive me for my unkindness, master. I did not mean it. Now quickly, you must summon rain. The tree will burn to cinders otherwise."

Oberon threw back his head, laughed wildly, and then coughed. "Let it. I don't care. Let fire cleanse this hateful place."

"Your fondness for symbolism aside, my liege, people *live* in that tree. You can't just burn it down because you want to prove a point."

"Oh, very well."

Tetchily, Oberon waved his arm. The thunder died down

immediately, and instead of lightning, the black clouds began to issue forth a deluge. The fire was extinguished in minutes.

☆☆☆

As Puck and Oberon landed on a nearby oak, it became clear that a good third of the leaves on Ariel's tree had been burned away.

"One of them might have been..." Puck trailed off.

"It doesn't matter," Oberon told him, coughing again. His lungs felt like an unswept hearth. "I've lived this long without them, after all."

Puck's lower lip trembled. "But you wanted them so much."

Then he folded both arms around Oberon's waist, pressing his face into his chest, and began to snuffle.

Oberon had no idea what to do. Generally speaking, his subjects did not make a habit of crying on him, much less crying in sympathy for his losses. He remembered that his father used to cry often, usually to get something he wanted, and would not stop until it was given to him. His mother had cried very seldom, usually only in the aftermath of Ariel's cruelties. Neither of them had ever turned to him for comfort, and Titania, as far as he could ascertain, never cried at all.

The fairy king racked his brains. He himself was prone to tears in the course of their more intense games, a fact he would have been hideously ashamed of had anyone in the world but Puck known it. On those occasions, Puck would lick them off his face, and then, putting aside whatever toy he'd been using to provoke them in the first place, he'd comb Oberon's hair or work it into a plait or simply massage his scalp.

So Oberon sunk his fingers into Puck's luscious black hair and tried to recall how to make a plait. It had been years since he'd had to style his own hair, and he didn't think he'd ever been called upon to style anyone else's. But surely, it couldn't be that difficult...

"Ow," said Puck, a moment later. "What in Hades's name are you doing?"

Frustrated, Oberon tugged at the tangled mess beneath him. "There's something wrong with your hair, sprite. It won't bend properly."

Puck laughed that particular throaty laugh of his, which Oberon knew to be his real one. To hear it was a privilege, as Puck had as many false laughs as there were ants in a hill.

"My sweet, incompetent master," he said, stroking his cheek. "When I get you home, I will teach you how to do it properly."

"And punish me for my follies?" Oberon asked, gruff and hopeful, covering Puck's hand with his own.

"Er...hello. Sorry, are you busy?" said Bunce, hovering nearby awkwardly. "I just wanted to check that you were both all right."

"Bunce!" Oberon cried, beaming.

His former lover smiled shyly. "Hello, Oberon. Pardon my haste, but Lord Ariel is currently seeing to his court. No casualties, as far as I can tell, but I think you should both leave now, while he's distracted. He's very angry."

Puck snorted regally. "My master does not flee from his enemies, he—"

"We flee," said Oberon, decisively, and scooped Puck up into his arms. "Where is the eagle?"

When Bunce lead them to it, Puck insisted he leave with them. The guard shook his head. "Thank you. But no. I told you, I like my work. It may not seem like much of a life to you, but it's important to me."

Puck looked up at Oberon beseechingly. But Oberon was, for once, ahead of him.

"Return to my court, and I will make you captain of my guard," he told Bunce. "Stay here, and Ariel will likely take his anger out on you. You know what cruelty he is capable of. My court is greater than his, and I can protect you."

"And we'll let you have the eagle. It's a mean-spirited bird, and I don't care for it," added Puck, and the eagle gave him a baleful look.

Bunce still regarded them hesitantly. "I wouldn't...complicate things, would I?"

"Isn't he dear?" said Puck. "Please say we can keep him, master."

Oberon stepped forward and pulled his first lover into a warm embrace. "No, my friend, you would not."

Soon, all three of them were flying back eastwards, the rising sun warming their faces, and Ariel's smouldering court far behind them.

Chapter Six

Despite the elation of their departure from Ariel's court, as soon as they returned home, Oberon went into mourning. While Puck introduced Bunce to Titania and her handmaidens, the king retired to his private quarters and remained there for days. He emerged only once or twice, shunning company in favour of wandering off on his own, often returning after dark and foregoing dinner.

"Really, isn't this a bit excessive?" asked Titania, exasperated. "He's been flightless for most of his life. He's managed well enough. It's not as though he's lost anything."

Puck was fond of Titania, but she had an unfortunate tendency to demand that the misery of others be logical. It was a vexing character flaw.

On the seventh day after their return home, Oberon sent Puck a letter. *Come* was all it said. When Puck presented himself at the door, Oberon dragged him inside, and quickly shut it behind him.

"I want your honest opinion," Oberon told him, striding across the room, while Puck settled hopefully on his bed. Going a week without sex had been a sore trial indeed, and whatever intrigue his master's strange behaviour might have provoked was inconsequential next to the desire to latch himself onto his cock like a limpet to a boulder. Moreover, during the seven days Puck had been prevented from performing his duties, Oberon had grown the beginnings of a fine beard. Very promising.

"Bunce is settling in well," he said as Oberon opened up his cupboard, blocking Puck's view of what was within it with his back. "I thought it strange at first, that you'd take to him. He hardly seems your type, even a younger you. But I imagine he was a welcome change, after Ariel. Kind and straightforward and honest. Not a player of games."

Puck's amiability towards their new captain of the guard was largely due to the way Oberon had greeted him. One look at his master's wide, genuine smile had been enough to convince Puck he had nothing to fear. He no longer loved Bunce in that way. It was a great relief, for Puck found much to admire in the guard and would have hated to have had to disembowel him.

"I never considered that. Perhaps you have a point. But it was his knowledge of poetry that first attracted me to him."

Puck smiled indulgently. "My master does like his poets."

"I do. In fact, that was what gave me the idea..."

With a flourish, Oberon turned and presented his surprise.

They were exquisitely crafted. Puck would not have thought Oberon's large fingers deft enough for the task, had he not personally experienced what those fingers were capable of. Like Puck's, they put one in mind of a butterfly—but while Puck's wings had ragged edges reminiscent of a comma, these more resembled the wings of a painted lady. They were off-white, similar in colour to...

"Paper?" said Puck.

"I tried other materials, but none were light enough. I used some of the poems you've given me in the past... after memorizing their contents, of course."

And, yes, now that Puck drew closer, he could see the prosthetic wings in Oberon's hands were decorated not with mere ornamental patterns, but with writing. *His* writing.

"They're beautiful," he breathed. "But do they..."

"They need to be sprinkled with dust. And I'm still working on the harness. But yes, they seem to work. Obviously, I can't flap, and I'll always be slow, but they'll get me off the ground. As long as it isn't raining."

"Try them on!" Puck begged. "I want to see!"

"Yes, yes. All in good time. But would my servant not prefer that I give him *his* present first?"

Puck's wings fluttered with excitement. "Ooh, what is it?"

Oberon smirked and stepped forward to loom over him. "Oil."

Shortly thereafter, Puck lay prostrate upon Oberon's feather bed, naked and with a jug of wine within arm's reach, while Oberon knelt beside him and massaged his back with oiled hands. Ah, to be pampered. He gave an appreciative rumble as Oberon's strong fingers ran down his trapezius, feeling a bead of warm oil trickle down to the base of his spine.

"It occurs to me, sprite, that although you now have all my dirty secrets in your possession, I still have little idea of *your* origins."

Puck knew this to be true. They'd met in the wilderness while Puck was scavenging for mushrooms small enough to fit in his cooking pot, and Oberon had never asked him why he lived alone, or where he'd come from, or why he didn't use his real name.

"I will tell you one day," Puck promised, although there was a part of his soul that quaked in fear of the day. Then his thoughts broke apart as Oberon undid a longstanding muscle knot. "*Nghhhuh.*"

"Oh," Oberon chuckled, his new beard scratching the back of Puck's neck as he buried in nose in his hair. "Did my servant like that?"

Puck swallowed, thickly, for a lump had appeared in his throat. Ever since meeting Ariel, he had marvelled that anyone who had grown up in a loveless world could be so good-hearted and sensuous. But he didn't want to spoil things with his soppiness, and so he said, "Merely surprised to learn of your competence in such a menial task, master. Did you practice your skills on Bunce?"

His attempt at goading fell flat as Oberon pressed his fingertips deep into his flesh, firmly massaging his longsuffering musculature. "Don't be mean-spirited, wastrel. I think you'll come to like him."

"I already do. It irritates me. It's so difficult to be jealous of people you like."

Whatever response Oberon might have offered was lost in Puck's next moan. Heat was pooling in his belly, and he felt his shaft thickening against the feathers. Truthfully, he felt *excellent*, better than he had in years. Whether it was the wine, or the oil, or the nearness of one who he cherished above all others, at the moment the burdens of the world seemed far away and inconsequential. He vaguely hoped Oberon might fuck him soon, but there was no great hurry.

"By all the gods, you're beautiful," Oberon breathed.

"Mm-hmm," he purred, not quite sure what he was agreeing with. Thinking had become a chore.

Oberon's fingers dug into his buttocks and raked up to the middle of his back, making him shudder and suck in air. His nipples had tightened to small pebbles, and pressing them into the bed produced a delicious warmth all down his front.

"I want to paint you," Oberon sighed. "Not paint a picture of you—paint on you. Would you like that? The tip of an ink brush tickling all your sensitive places? How you'd squirm."

Puck did so like it when Oberon indulged his creative side. But he was incapable of saying so because, at that moment, Oberon ran both oiled hands down his wings, palms flat. Purring, Puck leaned back into his touch, luxuriating in the sensation of Oberon mapping them slowly.

"So delicate," Oberon said, tapping out a rhythm on the tip of one wing that made Puck writhe. "So strong."

"Oberon," Puck rasped, "if your cock isn't in me *this minute*, I will depart immediately to seduce the eagle."

He craned his head back to watch as Oberon took himself in hand. It had not escaped Puck's notice that his master had a guilty fondness for watching himself masturbate. In fact, Puck himself would have been happy to lie there and watch the way Oberon's face grew slack as his grip tightened on his lovely cock. But he truly did want to be fucked. So, he scraped some of the oil off his skin and, reaching back, began preparing himself. Soon he had Oberon's full attention once again.

"Ready?"

"Now. *Now*, Oberon."

One of Puck's favourite things about the lengthy period of time it took Oberon to sink his cock into him was the way his hand would sometimes stray to Puck's neck. Their discrepancy in size was sufficient for Oberon's thumb and index finger to meet, and the reminder of how overpoweringly immense his master was always put fire in Puck's blood. Better yet, every now and then, Oberon would squeeze, momentarily cutting off his air, and when Puck was very lucky indeed the squeeze would coincide with a thrust of Oberon's hips. That meant that just as Puck needed to gasp or moan, he'd find his lungs empty, and there'd be a delicious moment of panic before Oberon slackened his grip.

There was, of course, pain. But Oberon was careful enough that it came in short, transient bursts, fading quickly so it seasoned his pleasure rather than diluted it. By the time Oberon first hit his prostate, Puck's cock was leaking onto the bed.

Barely conscious of anything other than *heat* and *want*, it took Puck a moment to realise Oberon was speaking, low and rough, into his ear.

"... never say that I was false of heart,

Though absence seem'd my flame to qualify

As easy might I from myself depart,

As from my soul, which in thy breast doth lie..."

"Oh, you bastard," Puck whined as Oberon took hold of his aching cock. After a few firm strokes, Puck could do nothing but lie whimpering and boneless, one side of his face pressed into the mattress. His mouth hung half-open, moisture pooling beneath it with every soft pant. And Oberon continued:

"That is my home of love; if I have ranged,

Like him that travels, I return again..."

Though he always started slow and mindful, eventually Oberon dispensed with gentleness and gripped Puck's hips tightly. The first hard thrust made Puck's vision swim; the second and third made him swear filthy oaths. He lost count after that. Oberon's elegant recital was reduced to snarls and base grunts, his huge, gorgeous body now coated all over in fairy dust. They came, at last, in the same moment, the cries of master and servant mingling together as Oberon buried himself to the hilt.

"...rest of it," Puck heard Oberon mumble some minutes later.

Exhausted, Puck draped himself over his master's sweat-slick chest. "Hmm?"

"Want you to hear the rest of it," Oberon murmured. "It's...it's for you. Your William helped me with the middle bits, but I came up with the last lines on my own.

Never believe, though in my nature reign'd
All frailties that besiege all kinds of blood,
That it could so prepost'rously be stain'd.
To leave for nothing all thy sum of good."

By now, his master was clearly near to being overcome with shyness, and he cleared his throat before stammering out the final words:

"For...for nothing this wide Universe I call,
Save thou, my rose; in it, thou art my all."

Puck kissed his mouth languidly. "Silly thing. Go and get my whip. I do believe it's time I administer your punishment."

Midsummer Court

Chapter One

"And what do *you* want?" Oberon demanded of the next supplicant.

In Puck's opinion, she didn't look as cowed as she should have, standing in the presence of her king. Few of them did. Oh, they went through the motions—approaching the throne with their wings down and their shoulders hunched, bowing obsequiously before presenting Oberon with their pleas. But there was a reason that whenever Titania went abroad to visit her relatives in the East, the throne room found itself knee deep in people who wanted things.

The reason, Puck thought, was nothing more or less than the fact that his master was known to be the softer of the court's reigning monarchs. Not that many would have thought so to look at him, seated in his throne of fox bones, his onyx-encrusted diadem and the black jewels on his fingers making him appear menacingly regal. Puck had chosen Oberon's adornments for exactly this purpose. He had noticed a disturbing trend of supplicants trying to flirt their way into the king's good graces and wanted to give them reason to think twice.

"Please, Your Majesty," the fairy maiden quavered on her knees before the throne. "I apologise for bothering you. My family has fallen on hard times, and I find I must, in humility and shame, request a loan."

"I see," said Oberon, his eyebrows arching severely. "What sort of loan are you in need of?"

"Only a small one, sire. Some nuts, a bit of dried meat, anything you might have to spare. Enough to last me until the baby's weaned. Then I'll be able to get back to foraging myself."

"You are married, I understand? To...what's his name...Mustardseed? He's a competent hunter. Why isn't he keeping your larder stocked while you contend with the child?"

"He's run off, sire. Found himself a goblin girl half his age. I'm all alone now, except for my sister."

Puck sat at the foot of Oberon's throne, playing cat's cradle and humming to himself. As one of Oberon's advisors, his proper place would have been standing behind the throne with his hands clasped and his expression blank. He'd done his best for the first hour; then boredom had overcome him. He'd started to fidget and then to make rude faces at the supplicants, before finally sitting down and nestling against Oberon's left calf. At least the reprimanding looks and occasional prods from Oberon's boot served to break up the monotony. By all the gods, governance was a tedious business when you got right down to it.

He listened as the maiden gave Oberon her story in more detail, a story which had much in common with those that had been offered up by the twelve supplicants who had preceded her. Beyond an errant partner, there was also the problem of a sister who gambled and a sickness in the child's stomach which was taking up all her time. Puck did not doubt that it was all true. He also did not doubt that had Titania been the one to receive her, the supplicant would not have sniffled and sighed half so often. It was well known that the queen had no patience for emotional excesses. Oberon, however... Oberon was a dear. Puck could see sympathy beginning to well up in the corners of his master's eyes, his expression softening as the list of her woes grew ever more heartrending.

When she was finished, Oberon sat with his thumb resting against his chin and his brow furrowed in thought, as though he hadn't already made his decision. Then: "Very well. Given that the circumstances you describe were beyond your control, the throne will loan you enough food to see your family through the next six months. You will meet tomorrow with one of my advisors so that together you may plan for winter and ensure that you do not find yourself in such a position again. As for your husband, I will send word to the goblin prince and have him retrieved. Upon his return, you may do what you like with him."

The supplicant burst into messy tears and departed, praising him to the heavens and back again.

Putting aside his string and tapping Oberon's leg, Puck whispered, "Master, that is the eighth loan you have granted today."

Oberon scowled at him. "What is your point?"

That if you keep going at this rate the throne will be bankrupt by the end of the week, Puck thought. Of course, he wouldn't dream of addressing Oberon thusly in front of the gathered supplicants and courtiers, and he had no wish to provoke a public quarrel. "No point, my liege, other than the observation that you are doing sterling work."

He made a mental note to arrange a placatory meeting with Redleaf, who managed the royal treasury and threatened either resignation or suicide once a month. Not that Puck would have minded all that much if he went through with either; Redleaf had had aspirations towards Oberon's bed before Puck's arrival, and even now, he tended to address the king with what Puck felt was an unseemly level of familiarity. That said, Titania would not be pleased to find her court bereft of a treasurer upon her return.

Before Oberon could turn away, Puck added, "I am obliged to remind you that the feast is in a few hours. We should depart soon if I am to get you ready in time."

The last sentence he said softly, allowing his tongue to flicker over his lips. That did the trick. Oberon's throat worked, and then he announced to the room at large in his booming voice that he would receive all remaining petitioners tomorrow. As he stood up from his throne, he offered Puck his hand. This was something that had only started happening quite recently, and Puck derived as much joy from the dozens of jealous glares he received as from the feeling of Oberon's warm skin sliding against his palm.

☆☆☆

"By the rank breath of Cerberus," Oberon proclaimed some ten minutes later, rubbing his brow. "How is it that I always forget how much Titania does?"

He sat sprawled in Puck's acorn chair, long legs splayed out so far they almost touched the opposite wall, while Puck prepared a restorative brew made from almonds and honey. They had adjourned to Puck's dwelling knowing that by now, Oberon's private quarters would be under siege by yet more supplicants.

"The queen is one of nature's administrators," Puck replied. "Believe me, master, she enjoys it."

"She has a better head for numbers than I," Oberon said, raising a goblet to his lips. After draining it, he assumed a threatening visage and added, "Don't think I didn't notice you rolling your eyes, sprite. Need I remind you that it is not your place to undermine my authority in front of the court, regardless of your opinion of my decisions?"

Puck inclined his wings in a show of submission. "My apologies, master. Your servant forgot himself."

Oberon didn't believe for a moment that that was an end of it. His Puck did not surrender so easily; later, he had no doubt, they were going to have one of those lengthy squabbles where Puck's agile tongue and wit tied Oberon's sound arguments in knots. Oberon suspected that the only reason he was getting off so lightly now was that Puck was aware of how frustrating and tiresome Oberon found governing in Titania's absence, and he was being merciful.

I am in love with a fiend, but a kind fiend, he thought. Placated, he accepted the apology and the kiss that accompanied it. "This feast... I suppose there's no way to get out of it?"

"I fear not. The court would consider it a bad omen if their king was not there to celebrate the solstice with them. Besides, I do think you'll enjoy it this year. We've arranged fire-dancers and a pixie choir, and there'll even be a cad-baiting before dessert. You love those."

"Cad-baiting" was a polite euphemism for a time-honoured fairy game, in which a mortal rapist was brought before the court, tied to a tree, and had sharpened sticks stabbed into their soft bits until the court grew bored and burned them alive. It was a splendid lark.

"Besides," Puck added, plucking the goblet from Oberon's fingers, "I'm sure I can improve my master's mood before we are due to arrive at the feast."

Oberon smirked. He had been thinking along the same lines. An hour spent reddening his servant's backside would do much to soothe his spirits. "In truth? And how do you…"

He started as a pair of arms belonging to someone standing *behind* him slid over his shoulders. Turning in his seat, he found himself gazing into the face of…Puck?

"Hello, master," the second Puck purred and licked at his slack mouth.

"What…you…" Oberon babbled, as a third Puck appeared at his right and sat down on his knee.

The first Puck stood with his arms folded and an air of supreme smugness. "A new trick I learned. Do you like them?"

The Puck in Oberon's lap had begun to remove his clothes, while the one behind him had already shed its own. Wanting to drink in the sight of both of them, Oberon tugged the second Puck down onto his right knee. "Are they real?"

Puck waggled his fingers. "That's a complicated question. They're me. Not copies, not puppets. More like reflections in a mirror. My thoughts are theirs, theirs are mine, anything you do to one of us you do to all of us. We'll become one person again in an hour or so."

"Most ingenious," said Oberon, touching this one's cheek, that one's chin, ascertaining that both reflections were solid and warm. "An hour, you say? Shall we move this to the bed?"

All three Pucks exchanged grins and, taking hold of his arms, hoisted him out of the chair. Unused to being manhandled, Oberon blinked as they pulled him across the room and pushed him down onto Puck's mattress of petals and dove feathers. Speedily, they divested him of the rest of his clothing, save for his diadem.

"Shall we tie his hands?" one of them asked the others. "He does look so handsome when he's helpless."

"Agreed," said the one coaxing Oberon's nipples into stiff rosy buds with his tongue. The other two set about drawing back Oberon's arms and securing them to the bedpost with strong ropes. Nothing he wouldn't be able to break free of if he tried, but that wasn't the point.

Much as he enjoyed the way the ropes bit into his flesh, what rapidly overwhelmed Oberon's senses was less the binding and more the presence of so much Puck. So much olive skin, so many silver wings, so many skillful hands running down his sides, his thighs, his chest. It was a welcome, if dizzying, reward for spending the last six hours with his arse glued to Titania's throne.

The Puck straddling his waist brushed his thumb over Oberon's lips, coaxing them to part before slipping two fingers into his mouth. Oberon rolled them underneath his tongue, suckled them as he would Puck's cock, and then, to be cheeky, he gave them a sharp nip.

All three Pucks squeaked, the top one gasping "Swine!" as he withdrew his fingers.

Smirking coquettishly, Oberon jerked his hips upwards, almost tossing them off him.

"Such insolence. Is this how my generosity is rewarded?" said the Puck on his left, smacking his face. "I can see that Titania's absence has caused you to get above yourself, Oberon. I have no choice but to remind you of your proper place through most severe punishment."

Oberon scoffed, concealing his glee. "Servant, you think you have the power to chastise me? There is less strength in your arm than in the least of my fingers. Do your worst."

Oh, that had been a mistake. The few times he had said those words in the course of their play, Puck's eyes had taken on a fell light, and what had followed had been...had been...

Perhaps I won't make it to the feast after all, Oberon thought, shivering happily.

"Watch him," the topmost Puck told the other two and hopped

off the bed while they did evil things to Oberon's nipples. Oberon heard him moving about the room, opening cupboards and drawers as though looking for something. Stalwartly, Oberon refrained from contemplating what it might be; he was painfully aroused by the identical beauties caressing his chest and his biceps, and wanted to draw things out as long as possible. History had proven that his body could be coaxed to completion by nothing more than his imagining whatever delights Puck had in store for him.

When the third Puck reappeared in Oberon's field of vision, he was holding a small black box. Intrigued, Oberon shuffled upwards, the bonds affording him just enough freedom of movement to lay his head back on the pillow so he could have a better view.

"Do you remember that conversation we had some weeks ago, my liege?" the Puck on his left inquired, nibbling on his ear.

"We have many conversations, beauteous and lovely youth."

"I felt that this one might have lingered in your memory," said the Puck on his right, kissing his neck. "We were down at the river. I was washing your hair. We were discussing the complex and troubling nature of bodies; the things they like, the things they don't like but want anyway, the things they like but don't want. In the course of our discussion, I told you an anecdote about a mortal couple I once knew, and a particularly intriguing game they used to play."

Oberon's breath caught in his throat.

"Now do you remember?" the Puck on the left whispered into his ear. Meanwhile, the third Puck had sat down on the edge of the bed, and opened up his black box. He waved his fingers over it, muttering a spell that Oberon recognized as the one that he used whenever he was about to give himself a new tattoo and needed to sterilize his implements.

Yes, Oberon remembered. He remembered listening to Puck's anecdote with amusement, and then shock, and then with an acute awareness of his own damp palms and a weakening sensation in his knees. He'd thought about it for days afterwards, and of course, Puck had known. His Puck always knew.

"Did you...did you make it yourself?" Oberon asked, his voice rough.

"I did. It took me ages—very delicate work—and I'm rather pleased with the result. I tested it on myself."

"Look how large his pupils have gone," said the Puck on Oberon's left, stroking his face.

"I'll get him some water," said the Puck on his right. A moment later, the rim of a silver cup was raised to Oberon's lips. The king's tongue was very dry, and he swallowed a mouthful gratefully.

As the third Puck came to lie on his belly between Oberon's legs, Oberon focused on the object in his hand, the object he had taken out of the black box. It didn't look like much, just a thin, plain silver rod, about the length of his hand.

"What do you think? Shall we give it a go?" all three of them whispered in unison.

"Yes," Oberon said, and they smiled. He added, "Cut the bonds first. I want my arms free."

The silver scissors that were always within arm's reach of the bed flashed, and the ropes fell away. Oberon placed an arm around the Puck on his left and another around the Puck on his right, and drew them in, in the way a child afraid of the dark might embrace favoured toys for comfort. They settled in against his chest, making reassuring noises.

The third Puck, however, was already intent on his task. Oberon was half-hard, trepidation slowing his body's responses to being fondled, and the king wondered if that might be a problem. Would the rod go in more easily if he was fully erect? Or would that increase the risk that it would get...that it would get *stuck*? He breathed deeply to calm his nerves and refrained from asking. His lover would know what he was doing.

Sensing his disquiet, the Pucks in his arms raked their fingers through his hair soothingly. The third, meanwhile, had dipped the rod in a small pot of oil, some of which he dabbed onto Oberon's slit. And then...then...

It didn't hurt, which surprised him. Perhaps it was simply the deftness of Puck's fingers, but the rod seemed to require no effort to insert. It slid in, bringing with it a strange, intimate sensation he couldn't put a name to. A slight pressure, a slight fullness, and *fuck*, now it was almost an inch deep.

It was the oddest thing, to be only half-erect and yet as aroused as he'd ever been in his life.

"Master?" inquired the Puck on his right.

Oberon realized that he'd been whimpering. He swallowed, feeling lightheaded, and became aware that his cheeks were wet.

Puck didn't move it any further in. Instead, he began to move it back and forth, with the same meticulous care that Oberon used when fucking his servant's tight, perfect body.

"I've tested it on myself several times now, actually," said the Puck on Oberon's right. "The last time, I got it quite deep, though—I wasn't measuring. I enjoyed the experience, and I wondered, what if I let it go? Let it sink all the way in, let it disappear? How would that feel? Would I be able to get it out again? What would happen if I came with it in..."

Oberon sobbed.

The Puck on his left chuckled, low and dark. "Another thought that occurred was what if I had it in me that deep, and then I let you bury yourself to the hilt in my arse? Would you be able to feel it?"

"Although, if I were to try that, we'd need a much longer rod," said the Puck on his right, as the silver rod slid relentlessly in and out of Oberon's cock. "Imagine, Oberon—watching it glide down into you and then disappearing..."

Oberon was breathing heavily, but none of it seemed to be reaching his lungs. His chest felt as though it was about to split open.

"Oberon?" said all three Pucks sharply, when he didn't reply.

"Stop," Oberon whispered.

Quick as a whip, the rod was withdrawn. The sudden sensation of emptiness was so vivid it took him back to the moment when Ariel had severed his wings. Squeezing his eyes shut, Oberon shuddered.

Then there were lips against his eyelids, his ears, and his jaw. Nimble fingers meandered down his chest, tracing gentle patterns in his skin. His servant's scent filled his nostrils, and he gathered all of them up in his arms.

"Forgive me," he said when he had control of his tongue. "I lost my nerve."

Blithe as a spring morning, the three of them laughed. One said, "Forgive what, master? You were beautiful."

"And so brave," added another, taking his hand and kissing the back of it. "You are not in pain?"

Oberon concentrated. His cock, now soft against his thigh, still felt miserably empty, and tender, but not sore. "No, not at all. I liked it. I loved it. I want to do it again. Can we, my sprite?"

"Mmm. Whatever you like, my king."

All three of them were rubbing themselves against him like attention-starved cats. Now with his wits about him, Oberon reflected on what it might feel like for Puck to come three times, and all at once.

"What*ever* I like, is it...?" he purred.

Chapter Two

By the time they departed for the feast, the wind had picked up and grey clouds hovered overhead.

"Take care, master," Puck said, helping Oberon with the harness. "I know you've spent months mastering your technique, but this weather is treacherous."

"Bah. Don't be a nursemaid. If a mere breeze can best me, I don't deserve to fly at all."

The journey, short as it was, proved a challenge; his prosthetic wings did not afford him the same measure of control over his trajectory as his real ones had. At one point, he almost glided into a tree. More troublesome was the fact that the gale was intensifying, and when they arrived at the ancient cave, in which the feast was to take place, it was starting to rain.

Although Oberon's landing was imperfect, his arrival was greeted with thunderous applause from the revelers. He bowed, basking in their approval. *Gods, I love being a king.*

"Well done," Puck whispered as he led him to his seat. He helped him take off the wings and put them safely to one side, for the harness wasn't comfortable for long periods.

It didn't escape Oberon's notice that Puck drew many an appreciative eye. Unsurprising, as he looked good enough to eat. He'd painted his naked torso with red berry juice, so from across the room it looked as though he were wearing some gauzy, skintight material. He'd grown his hair out for the occasion, and his curly black locks touched his shoulders, many of them decorated with gold coins that jingled when he turned his head.

Such shameless vanity, thought Oberon, his chest warm with adoration.

All nine hundred members of Oberon's court were in attendance that evening, as well as a dozen guests. The lichen-stained walls were hung with hundreds of will-o'-the-wisps, and the cold cave floor was covered with the skin of a red fox. Incense jars were posted at regular intervals around the perimeter like sentinels, imbuing the air with a spicy, alluring scent that mingled with the smell of roasted mushrooms, grilled lizard meat, and wine as the food was brought in. As was customary, Oberon toasted his absent queen's chair, and the feast began in earnest.

An hour later, Oberon had to concede that he was enjoying himself. The entertainment had lived up to Puck's promises—the pixies had been met with thunderous applause, and the cad's corpse, unrecognizable as a man, had been removed before it started to smell. Better yet, Puck's hand had spent the majority of the evening resting on Oberon's knee. The king had thought that Puck might try to tease him to completion in the course of the meal, for his servant was always ready to capitalize on Oberon's exhibitionist tendencies. To his surprise, Puck behaved himself, only now and then stroking Oberon's thigh. As Oberon partook of his third cup of wine, he reflected upon his blessings.

The storm had gathered strength as they ate. Titania's seneschal had had the foresight to hang branches, fabrics, and a tough, broad piece of deer hide over the entrance to the cave to block out the sound of the tempest. Even so, now and then, there would come a loud crack of thunder, and Oberon saw a few of his subjects glancing toward the cave entrance.

Puck leaned across and said, "Master, should I go see to the river? I set wards in place to prevent it from bursting its banks earlier, but they might be taking strain."

"Don't be absurd, sprite. You can't go out in this; your wings will soak in seconds. I shall go. You keep the court entertained in my absence."

"Very well," Puck mumbled with obvious reluctance, taking his cape.

After being dogged at every turn by courtiers, supplicants, and advisors for the past week, it was a great relief to Oberon to note that most of the revelers were so inebriated they didn't seem to notice his departure. Pulling aside the deer hide and stepping out into the storm, Oberon took a deep breath, as rain slammed into his front and sides. Since childhood, he had loved tempests, even those not of his making. This one had been brewing for some days, prickling the back of his consciousness with anticipation.

He wanted to run, so he discarded his diadem and leapt into the undergrowth. Such was the ferocity of the storm that even sucking in a lungful of air was a challenge, and when he reached the river, he was panting and soaked to the bone. The earth beneath his bare feet was deliciously wet, and he extended his arms to the heavens and let the wind wrap itself around his body like a lover.

Duty called. Oberon's court made its home in a shadowy glade ringed by alders and oaks. Crossing it required a short jog, and the river lay to its left, a five-minute run from Oberon's throne room. Careful inspection revealed that Puck's wards were holding up well; the river would not burst its banks this night. Satisfied, Oberon headed back to the feast, his mind on the strawberry trifle.

Midway through the glade, he stopped when a distant rumbling sound reached his ears. Looking back curiously, he found a wall of mud bearing down on him.

☆☆☆

"Go on," Puck whispered. "She's been eyeing you all evening. Such quavering is unseemly in a man of arms."

Bunce fiddled with his cutlery as though it were much more intriguing than the young lady who was shooting him yet another flirtatious smile from across the room. Peaceblossom was one of Titania's handmaidens. She had an interesting countenance, the top half comprised of delicate, doll-like features: a petite nose; a golden, curling fringe; and gently sloping eyebrows. Her jaw, by contrast, was solid and square, and her hair was chopped short. The overall effect was arresting, and beautiful in a peculiar way.

"She's been eyeing *you*," Bunce insisted.

"Nonsense. They've all lost interest in me. I'm too familiar now. You are the court's latest fascination. 'Who is this mysterious and strapping newcomer, whom Oberon has made captain of the guard?' they ask themselves. 'Is he married? Does he want to be?'"

"Are you making fun of me, Mister Goodfellow?" said Bunce, with playful sternness. Then he paled and ducked his head, muttering, "Oh, ten hells, she's looking this way again."

Unbeknownst to Bunce, it was Puck who had drawn Peaceblossom's attention to him in the first place. Like her mistress, Peaceblossom was an inveterate gambler, and he often met with her to play cards. Upon hearing that she had discarded her latest lover, Puck had made much of Bunce's qualities and of the new captain's loneliness since arriving at Oberon's court, for he knew Peaceblossom to have a kind and piteous heart. It was one of the many reasons Puck thought they would make a good match.

"Go and ask her for a dance, you oaf. Why do you think she's wearing that elaborate girdle? That's all for your benefit. Show her your appreciation."

At that moment, the chatter and laughter of the feasting court was cut off by a low rumble that quickly rose to a roar. The cave trembled, sending plates to the floor and knocking dancers off their feet. Then, just as abruptly, all went quiet.

"An earthquake?" Puck wondered, standing to see if anyone was injured.

"A mudslide, I'd wager," said Bunce.

They looked at one another and said, "Oberon."

Bunce jumped onto the table and barked, "All guards, to me. The king is in danger. Everyone else, remain here, please."

A low buzz filled the cave as twenty pairs of wings began vibrating, and Bunce's new troops arranged themselves in formation.

It took a moment, as most of them were tipsy. Privately, Puck couldn't help but feel that Bunce would command more authority if he were not compelled to tack a "please" on to the end of every order.

Puck pointed at two of his own personal minions. "You. Come."

They obeyed, assisting Puck in enacting the spell required to keep the guards' wings dry in the rain. As they left the cave with Bunce in the lead, Puck summoned several dozen fireflies to hover alongside them, for the moon was smothered by storm clouds.

In his heart, Puck was not that afraid for his king. He knew Oberon had survived far worse than mudslides. What did make his brow furrow was the thought of how much damage had been done to the glade. His fears were not allayed by the realization that although they were now flying directly over the spot the court's dwelling should have occupied, he couldn't see any of it—only a vast lake of mud and rubble.

"Puck, look. The hill," said Bunce.

Even in the dim light, Puck could see that the tall hill which loomed over the glade was now missing a chunk of its side, as though a giant had taken a bite out of it.

"Praise be to Persephone that everyone was at the feast," Bunce murmured. "Have you ever seen such chaos? It'll take us months to clear all this mess out."

Puck ignored him, scanning the ground for any sign of Oberon. A sickly feeling was developing in his gut, as it occurred to him that even one as strong and hardy as his master might well suffocate if trapped under all this earth. Lacing his fingers together, he mumbled an incantation for a spell he had created last summer. Its purpose had been to aid Oberon on his hunting expeditions by identifying those patches of ground under which badgers and other burrowing things lurked.

"There!" he shouted a moment later, pointing to a spot close to the tree that housed the court's famous weaver's nest. "All of you, dig! Now!"

"Must we?" asked Cobweb, the more fastidious of his minions, as

Bunce's troops rushed downwards. "Wouldn't it be faster if you unearthed him with your sorcery?"

Puck took hold of his neck and hissed, "My sorcery is not unlimited, and I may need to use some of it to restart our master's heart. Dig, you worse than senseless thing!"

Some artistic license there—if Oberon's heart had stopped, the badger-hunting spell would not have worked. Nevertheless, it did the trick. Cobweb gulped and hastened to join the diggers.

The mud had not yet hardened, and it didn't take two dozen pairs of hands long to create a deep trench. The further down they dug, the more Puck became aware of the scale of the devastation. The only homes that had been spared were those that had been built in the uppermost thirds of the trees, and those were few in number; it was considered safer to settle close to the ground, where there was less wind to batter your dwelling and fewer birds to make a meal of you. Titania's private suite was submerged, as were the royal storehouses where all their winter provisions were squirreled away amidst the roots of a great oak. The throne room, hidden from mortal eyes in a cluster of densely packed mulberry bushes, was destroyed. Oberon's private quarters had been spared by lucky chance; a boulder had shielded the yew in which they resided from the worst of the avalanche.

So much to rebuild. Where do we even start? Puck thought, his heart aching. Oberon's court was the first real home he'd ever known. Prior to his arrival, he'd lived a nomadic existence, rarely staying in one place for more than a month, and assumed himself incapable of forming an attachment to any one location. *How time changes us.*

From the bottom of the freshly dug pit, a glint of silver caught his eye.

"Here!" called one of the diggers, and they renewed their efforts with fervour. A lock of hair was joined by an ear, and then an arm, and then the mud heaved upwards. Like a monster arising from an ancient swamp, Oberon pulled himself free of a coffin of wet earth and staggered to his feet. The cheers of the diggers turned to cries of dismay as he collapsed the next instant, falling against the slippery wall of the pit.

"Out of my way," Puck snapped at the diggers, pushing them aside in his haste to get to the king, every inch of whom was coated with mud. His breathing was ragged, and as Puck approached, he coughed up what seemed to be a lungful of water and gravel.

"Hold on to me, master." Arms around his waist, Puck drew him up, wings beating with such force that three of the diggers were buffeted to the bottom of the pit themselves.

Once they were clear of the pit, he placed Oberon on the ground and patted his back as he coughed up more mud. Bunce landed beside them, wringing his hands and prattling half-formed enquiries as to Oberon's health.

"What...what happened?" Oberon managed, at last.

"There was a mudslide, my liege. The whole glade is submerged."

"Couldn't you wait a few minutes before telling him that?" Bunce scolded.

Puck ignored him, preoccupied in brushing enough dirt away so as to allow him to make certain that Oberon had sustained no serious injuries. The rain had stopped, and as Oberon wiped mud from his eyes, he got his first proper look at the chaos, and swearing, he leapt to his feet.

"Is anyone trapped?" he demanded of Bunce.

"My guards have done a headcount. The only members of the court not still at the feast are ourselves."

"Call them all here at once. All those who aren't completely drunk, at any rate. We need to excavate as much as we can before the mud hardens." As soon as Oberon finished speaking, he fell prey to another coughing fit.

As the immensity of their task became apparent, Puck thought longingly of the strawberry trifle waiting uneaten back at the feast. He then said to the onlookers, "You heard the king. Hop to it!"

Chapter Three

Morning revealed the full extent of the disaster.

The greater part of the glade was under at least six feet of mud. A third of the trees in which Oberon's court made their homes had been toppled. Large boulders had been thrown down the hill, crushing many delicate structures that had been built on the ground. There were a few small mercies: the storm had cleared up, although there wasn't a slice of blue sky to be seen in any direction yet; and the wind that had spent the last several hours assaulting their ears finally died down. Oberon's pet foxes were alive, safe in their den, and his falcon was found sulking on a tree not far away. Bunce had flown up to the newly scarred hill, and ascertained that another avalanche was unlikely. Even so, Puck had given him spells to reinforce it.

These were all cold comforts to those who now found themselves faced with the task of digging up all their worldly possessions one by one. As a species, fairies were not naturally inclined towards long, boring, grimy jobs with little reward at the end of them. In most courts Puck had known, the victims of such a disaster would have taken one look at the task ahead of them and unanimously decided to seek out a new home. But this was Titania's court, and Oberon's court. The former's steady governance and the latter's force of personality had bred a loyal citizenry. They had rallied. There were five well-organized bucket chains at work, and a stream of younger fairies flying overhead, bringing water and tools to the workers.

"This *would* happen while Titania was away," said Oberon as they inspected the damage together.

He hadn't washed off the mud or, for that matter, sat down since being unearthed. Puck wanted to drag him down to the river or, better yet, into a hot bath. Knowing he wouldn't allow it, instead Puck handed him a cup of cold tea he'd procured from the remains of the abandoned feast. "Come, now. Surely you can't imagine she'll blame you for this?"

"The last thing she said to me before she left was 'I hope I shall return to find my court in one piece'," Oberon grunted. "I'll be damned lucky if she even gives me a chance to proffer an explanation before pulling out my eyes."

As usual, Puck thought, his master's perception of the queen's character was distorted by the lens of a millennia-old dead marriage. While Titania was quick-tempered and intolerant of folly, she was not half so unreasonable as Oberon implied.

To add to their woes, even though the clouds were slow to disperse, the weather turned uncommonly humid. By midmorning, the diggers were damp with as much sweat as mud, and by midday, the air was stifling. Reluctantly, Oberon called the work to a halt.

"You've done well," he said to the exhausted members of his court. "Rest for a few hours. We will begin again when the sun touches the horizon."

"My liege," said Titania's handmaiden Peaceblossom, approaching him with a bow. Sensibly, she had abandoned her gaudy girdle in favour of a leaf tunic, the edges of which she clasped as she spoke. "As you requested, I've assembled some preliminary notes on our food and supplies."

"And?"

"Three of our underground storerooms are still inaccessible, their entrances blocked by fallen rocks. Of those that have been unearthed, two have caved in, and only a third of their stores are salvageable. At the moment, I'd say that we've lost about half of our supplies overall. I won't be able to give you a more accurate estimate until the excavation is completed."

"With all the rebuilding, we'll not have much time to restock before the weather turns cold," said Oberon. "We're in for a hard winter, though a survivable one. Thank you, Peaceblossom. Your efforts are appreciated."

Despite the lightness of his tone, the king looked bleak. Excusing them to Peaceblossom, Puck took his arm and drew him away from the public's gaze.

He was unsure, at first, of where to go, for many of their usual private spaces were either submerged or destroyed. Upon reflection, Puck selected the safe, hidden spot behind the waterfall, which no one knew of but he. Pushing Oberon through the sheet of water helped to remove the hardened mud, and once they were alone in the dark cave beyond it, Puck brought out his best razor.

"You need a shave, master," he said in response to Oberon's quizzical look. "As charmingly rugged as you look, I prefer kissing skin to stubble."

Oberon shook his head and remained silent while the razor glided over his jaw. When Puck was done, he took out his silver scissors. His hands flew like the wings of sparrows, raking out knots and then snipping away split ends.

"It's important that your people see their king at his best in troubled times," Puck said, blowing away a cloud of silver hairs. Oberon grunted; Puck couldn't tell whether the sound indicated agreement.

When his hair had been returned to a semblance of tidiness, Oberon got to his feet, his movements slow and restrained, which Puck recognized as a sure sign of exhaustion on his master's part. Then, without a word, he placed his hands on Puck's shoulders, pushed him back against the mossy rock wall, and sank to his knees.

"That's very kind of you, master...are you sure you want to do this now, though?"

"No talking," Oberon muttered, undoing the knot on Puck's belt. "Not now. Please."

Puck, who had never been good at making love quietly, bit his lip and forced his tongue to lie still. Truth be told, he was also bone-tired, and much as he wanted to comfort his master, he wasn't sure his exhausted body would cooperate.

He had forgotten that Oberon had been honing this particular skill since long before Puck had had his first kiss. In a handful of minutes, his sharp canines and warm tongue had Puck's cock red and throbbing, and Puck's vow of silence fell to bits.

"Oh, this was such a good idea," he groaned, as Oberon's silver hair tickled the inside of his thighs.

In response, Oberon grabbed hold of Puck's hips and lifted him from his feet as he took his cock all the way down his throat. Bracing himself against the cave wall, Puck slid both legs over Oberon's broad shoulders. Now that his master's hands were no longer busy holding him up, they set about fondling his arse.

Neither of them were at their best, and it was a far clumsier exchange than their usual loveplay. Oberon didn't tease him, and Puck didn't try to last as long as he could. When he came down Oberon's throat, it was less like the anticipated ascent into celestial ecstasy and more like the painful relief of pulling a thorn from his foot.

When he slithered down to return the favour, he found that Oberon hadn't even stiffened.

"No, don't try," said the king, drawing Puck into his lap. "Kiss me. That's all I want for now."

Puck obliged. Oberon's mouth tasted of his seed, and his skin smelt faintly of rainwater. More than anything, Puck wanted to open his eyes and find that they were still curled up in his bed, and the last day and night had been a horrid dream.

When they parted, Oberon said, "Come. There's much to be done."

That evening, as the work began anew, the atmosphere in the glade was lighter. The setting sun cast a peach-coloured glow over those trees that were still standing, and hundreds of fireflies were called out to keep the diggers company. The children sang as they worked, and a bonfire was lit in the centre of the excavated area, where nuts and vegetables were roasted and distributed to anyone who hadn't eaten.

Puck spent half his time apportioning small allotments of magic here and there—when there was a boulder too large for the diggers to move, or when someone sprained their back trying to lift too heavy a load. The other half, he spent with a lengthy strip of parchment in his hands, rearranging Oberon's schedule for the next few days. A visit from the elves was postponed. A meeting with the royal treasurer was pushed back a month. His majesty's inspection of an old oak whose habitability had been in question could be put off indefinitely now that the tree had been swept away on the river of mud.

Oberon, meanwhile, put his considerable strength to good use. Once given a sturdy shovel, he sped up the excavation considerably; not only could he dig twice as fast as most other fairies thanks to his size, but Puck suspected that the sight of his bare chest rising and falling and glistening with sweat provided the court with a much-needed morale boost.

Chapter Four

As night drew in, the issue of accommodation reared its ugly head.

"Mighty Oberon, how can you ask this of us?" demanded a matronly fairy about the age of Oberon's mother. She stood at the head of a cluster of fourteen other well-dressed fairy men and women, most of them highly ranked members of court and all of them Titania's relatives.

Keep your temper, Oberon told himself. "Baroness, what would you have me do? Your homes lie beneath several hundred pounds of mud. Even if you could get to them, you wouldn't want to spend the night in them."

With the hand not grasping his shovel, Oberon gestured towards the sturdy oak on whose branches tents were being strung up and tiny lamps were being hung. "The weather will be good tonight, I am sure of it. You and everyone else will be perfectly safe from..."

"The weather? My liege, I don't care about the *weather*. I may be no spring chicken, but I don't tremble at the prospect of being rained on. No, my liege, the problem is this: my friends and I have inspected the particular branch upon which we are expected to lodge for the night. Frankly, it's unacceptable."

She folded her arms as murmurs of agreement rose up around her. They were powerful arms; despite her age, Baroness Mint was one of Oberon's finest hunters, skilled with bow and with blade. Even so, Oberon observed that she was still wearing her white gloves from the feast, and that they didn't have a spot of mud on them.

"Why, good lady?"

"To start with, it's one of the lowest branches. If I sleep on it, I shall spend the night staring up at the dirty feet and undergarments of the many hundreds of individuals snoring above me."

"I would have thought that you would find that preferable to being on a higher branch and having however many hundreds are below you staring up at your own…"

She interrupted him. "*Secondly*, my friends and I are expected to share the branch with our servants and their families. Why? Why can't they have their own branches?"

"The tree's branches are finite in number. More to the point, the arrangement has been made, and reorganizing everyone now would take time and effort that no one has to spare. Baroness Mint, if the accommodation provided is so wholly unacceptable to you, why don't you make your own arrangements? There are other trees. The forest is vast; you could sleep anywhere."

And hopefully get eaten by an owl, he thought. It wasn't vain hope. One of the reasons fairies lived in close-knit communities was that on their own they made a tasty snack for predators who saw them as hairless field mice.

"Don't be absurd, my liege," the baroness said, thrusting out her bosom and fanning her turquoise wings. "We cannot be seen abandoning the court in this time of trouble. The common folk look to us for inspiration and reassurance."

Enough of this. I have better things to do than quibble with a malcontent. "Baroness, I feel you are being unreasonable. Nonetheless, I do not wish you to endure more hardship than you already have. There are several dwellings that, by lucky chance, were left relatively unscathed by the mudslide; mine is one of them. Would you or any of your friends like to shelter there for the night?"

Gasps rippled through the group. Oberon heard one of those standing at the back whisper to his companion, "His home? His *bed*? Where he and that foreigner…?"

"You do not have to use the bed," Oberon ground out, his fists clenching. "Although I assure you it is clean. The floor is also perfectly comfortable, as is…"

"No," said the Baroness, backing down. "Your offer is kind, sire.

I think, however, that my friends and I will make do with our branch."

As they left, Oberon hoisted his shovel to continue digging and saw that it was broken; without his noticing, his grip had snapped it in half. Cursing, he went in search of another one.

Gods, I loathe being a king.

☆ ☆ ☆

Neither Puck nor Oberon retired until the full moon was high overhead. At last, so weary he could barely walk, never mind fly, Puck followed the king to his dwelling in the yew. His own home in the stout willow had also been spared, but he'd surrendered it to Bunce for the night. The captain's burrow was no longer fit for habitation, and the last time Puck had seen him, he'd looked even worse than Oberon, on the verge of collapse from sheer exhaustion.

As soon as Puck shut and locked the door behind them, Oberon fell face-first onto the bed and stopped moving. Puck's attempts to poke and prod him onto his side provoked only a series of snuffling noises. Eventually, Puck gave up and used Oberon's back as his mattress.

"Good night, master," he slurred and fell asleep.

☆ ☆ ☆

When he awoke to the smell of warm bread, Puck assumed it was a dream. Bread was a mortal luxury. Most fairies had never tasted it, and only a handful knew how to make it. Although Puck had acquired a rabid love of the stuff on one of his first jaunts to the human world, he had long since accepted the impossibility of incorporating it into the court's diet on a regular basis.

He kept his eyes shut, hoping to sustain the dream for as long as possible. As the smell grew stronger, and the saliva gathering in his mouth felt increasingly real, he tentatively opened one eyelid. Then he sat up with a squeal of delight.

"So I did do it right, then," said Oberon, sounding smug. He sat on the edge of the bed, a tray resting on his knees. On it, there were four thick, uneven slabs of bread, their edges browned and steaming, and beside them Puck spied two pots – honey and butter. "I wasn't sure how it was supposed to be prepared. Bunce suggested boiling it, but we couldn't find a pot. I remembered Titania's mother once telling me that almost all foods are improved by fire, so I ended up toasting it."

By the time he had finished speaking, Puck was halfway through the largest slab. The crunch of the crust made his toes curl. *Thank all the gods for mortals.*

Clearly amused, Oberon continued, "As to how I got hold of it... Yesterday, I sent out three teams of foragers to begin the task of replenishing our supplies. One team returned an hour ago, bearing a variety of strange goods, including a loaf of bread. They encountered a mortal merchant who had lost his way in the woods and redirected him onto the proper path in exchange for some of his wares. In addition to the loaf, we now possess a dozen potatoes, a round of cheese, six onions, and a pouch full of something called 'pepper'. Hardly enough to last us through winter, but a good start."

"What an affable and fortuitous exchange," said Puck with patent suspicion as he dipped his breakfast in honey. "If only all the court's encounters with mankind were so mutually beneficial."

It was a sad truth that many fairies regarded humans as savage animals—perhaps unsurprising, given the only representatives of the species most of them encountered on a regular basis were the cads who were hunted down for solstice celebrations. When a member of Oberon's court came upon a human in the wilderness, they would often play tricks on it; putting pebbles in its shoes, tying its hair in knots, or stealing items of clothing. Those who knew magic might conjure up illusions of wolves or bears and chase the luckless human until it either reached shelter or died of exhaustion. On occasion, a few would try to find out what human meat tasted like. Humans were not much better; if one came upon a fairy too weak or too slow to evade them, they tended to react by either stepping on them or trying to put them in a bottle to show to their children.

Oberon replied, "I made it known that anyone who prioritized their resentment of the mortals over our need for supplies and provoked a fight with them would be deemed a traitor and tried accordingly. And their empty bellies probably helped to ensure their good behavior."

Nodding in approval, Puck swallowed another mouthful of delicious toast. "Won't you try some, my liege?"

Oberon made a face. "No. It looks unhealthy. However..."

Leaning down, he licked the lingering traces of honey and butter from Puck's fingers and then from his mouth.

"When you're ready, sprite, duty calls," he said, standing.

In a perfect world, Puck would have thanked Oberon for his gift by upending the pot of honey all over his cock and then cleaning up every last drop with his tongue. As they had a full day's work ahead of them, he contented himself with giving Oberon's left buttock a pinch, and then he scampered from the room before Oberon could exact vengeance.

Puck's morning was given over to a thousand mundane tasks. He was called upon to settle a quarrel provoked by those members of the court whose homes had not yet been unearthed, and who complained that others were getting preferential treatment.

Then there were those who considered preferential treatment their due—friends and relatives of the queen, for the most part. They had put down their spades after half an hour's work and given the rest of their allotted digging time to their servants. He frightened them into submission with threats of turning their children into frogspawn.

At about midday, Bunce flew up to him, smiling.

"Good news, my friend!" said the captain, waving a battered piece of mulberry leaf upon which Puck could make out the queen's distinctive handwriting. "Titania has concluded her business abroad and will be returning in three days' time!"

Puck groaned. "Oh, Hades' frozen bollocks. That's all we needed."

He sought out Oberon and found him standing alone by the river's edge, resting his weight on his shovel and looking troubled.

"I take it you've heard, then?" Puck asked, landing beside him. "It's a blow, I'll admit. Don't worry overmuch though, master. As I've said, Titania will..."

"Titania?" the king barked, shaking his head as though coming awake all at once. "What about her?"

"Ah. You've not heard, then. All right. Don't be upset. Titania is coming home early. She will be here in three days."

All across the valley, birds took flight at the fairy king's despairing scream.

☆☆☆

"Better now?" Puck asked, ducking as Oberon's shovel was flung into the nearest tree.

"A week," Oberon groaned, his face in his hands. "That was all I needed. One more week, and we'd have made it. She wouldn't have been able to tell anything had happened."

Puck rubbed his back. "Don't be silly. Even if we'd cleared away all the mud in a week, we'd still have months of work ahead of us before the court returned to normalcy. Not to mention the matter of our diminished supplies."

"Yes, yes. You speak sense."

"Master, it seemed to me that you were perturbed before I brought you this news. Has something else happened?"

Oberon sighed, not wanting to add to Puck's burdens by sharing his own. "Not really. Nothing that matters."

Puck nodded placidly. Then, wings fluttering, he leapt into the air and came down on Oberon's shoulders, taking hold of two locks of his hair as though they were the reins of a horse. Tugging on them, he chanted, "Tell me, tell me, tell me, tell me..."

As Oberon snarled and tried to pull him off, Puck clenched his thighs around his master's neck, making himself impossible to dislodge. Undeterred, Oberon collapsed to the ground and rolled about like a man trying to extinguish a fire in his clothing. Puck hung on tight, even as grass and dirt got in his hair and smudged his wings.

"You are the most irritating thing that exists," Oberon said, seething, and Puck cackled.

Athletically, Oberon arched his back and then performed a perfect handstand. Now clinging upside down, Puck's blood rushed to his head.

"Clever," he rasped, clinging like a limpet. "Can you outlast me, I wonder?"

Oberon shot him a feral grin and maintained the handstand. It took four minutes for Puck to grow dizzy enough to moan and drop off, at which point the king fell upon him. With lightning speed, Oberon pinned his wrists and used his weight to keep the rest of him immobile.

"For that, I shall not let you have any more bread, brat," Oberon told him.

Going limp, Puck threw his head back and wept fat crocodile tears. Satisfied, Oberon was about to smother his cries with a kiss when he heard a faint gasp. Looking up, he saw that Peaceblossom was hovering overhead, wide-eyed, pink spots on her pale cheeks.

"I...oh...I apologise, I..." she stammered and flew away as fast as she could.

The two of them stared after her and then at one another before succumbing to hysterical laughter.

"Oh gods," Oberon said in between snickers, a hand over his face. "That'll power the gossip mill for the next three years."

It wasn't that their relationship was any great secret, however many members of the court might politely feign ignorance. In Oberon's opinion, it didn't even qualify as scandalous. Those rulers and royal consorts who had preceded Titania and Oberon had often had droves of lovers—some had even shared Oberon's proclivities so far as gender was concerned. Even so, both of them were well aware that in the comparatively short space of time since Puck had become a fixture at court, his constant presence at Oberon's side had caused tongues to wag. Wasn't it strange, they murmured, that his majesty would lavish so much attention on a servant, when he couldn't even muster up the enthusiasm to impregnate his own wife? And why had his majesty chosen a *foreigner* for a plaything, when there were so many handsome young lads available locally? And where, in fact, had Robin Goodfellow come from, and why did he never talk about his origins?

His arms now free, Puck linked them around Oberon's neck. "Master, what was troubling you earlier? Tell Puck so that he can fix it."

Oberon sighed. "As I said, I doubt there's anything to it. A short while ago I overheard Titania's second cousin—Cobweb, you know, the one with the nose?—speaking to Baroness Mint. They were discussing our recent catastrophe, and one of them raised the notion that the hill's collapse is a sign that the gods no longer favour us. That it is a punishment."

"A punishment? For what, pray?"

"Several potential crimes were postulated. The court's pride. The queen's gluttony. The one they eventually settled on was my deviancy."

Puck digested this. "By which I presume they were referring to..."

"My apparent inability to conceive a child and my relationship with you."

"I see. Please get off me, my liege. I have urgent business to attend to."

"Puck," Oberon said sternly. "We have discussed this. At my court, there are laws. You are not allowed to simply slit the throats of anyone you don't like."

"Why not? I *want* to," Puck whined, wriggling beneath him.

"Murder does not solve everything, my Puck."

"Oh, it does, master. Provided you keep at it for long enough."

When Oberon sighed again, Puck kissed his cheek. "However, if it means so much to you, I will refrain from dismembering your enemies. Provided, of course, their offences remain limited to slander."

They both knew that this was a weasel's promise. Oberon's court was home to some of the brightest and most ambitious of their kind. When a courtier took it into his or her head that either of their monarchs was no longer satisfactory, they progressed from harsh words to harsh deeds in the twinkling of an eye; defending Oberon's person from assassins was one of Puck's routine duties. In fact, it was hardly necessary, as Oberon had been shrugging off attempts on his life long before Puck's arrival, but it gave Puck the opportunity to indulge his secret sweet tooth for violence.

Nonetheless, Oberon accepted the promise with a nod and then said, "Well, sprite, you have brought me bad news and distracted me from my labors. So long as you're down there you might as well make up for it."

☆☆☆

Reinvigorated by the prospect of their queen's imminent return, the diggers put their shoulders to the wheel. In two days, a pathway had been cleared through the heart of the glade. Tall banks of mud still loomed on either side, but now that they could clearly see how far down it went and thus track their progress, the court attacked them with renewed vigor.

"We might make it," muttered Oberon, still holding out hope of concealing the event from Titania—although, in his heart, he knew it was unlikely. Even with the bulk of the mud shifted, there was a layer of grime on everything that hadn't been simply crushed in its wake. Every hand not wielding a shovel now carried a mop or bucket or polishing rag. Most unpleasantly, now and then they came upon the rotting corpse of some beast unfortunate enough to have been caught in the hill's collapse. Baroness Mint herself had found a desiccated skunk blocking the front door to her dwelling, and Oberon had been so busy over the last two days that he hadn't yet found time to ask Puck how he'd done it.

Otherwise, the king was satisfied with their progress. His subjects were turning out to be hardier than he would have expected, and he was proud of them. It was an unusual feeling. He'd strived all his life to avoid emulating his father, who seemed to regard all those he ruled with faint contempt. Oberon's sentiments towards his own court were dominated by affection and fear; it was like being the custodian of a large and delicate piece of artwork that required constant maintenance. Valuable as such a work might be, one would never think it to be of much practical use.

To find out how wrong he had been in his assessment of his subjects was humbling and gratifying.

"My liege, Peaceblossom asked me to bring you her latest assessment of the court's economic forecast," said Bunce, bowing as he landed and thrusting a piece of parchment at Oberon.

Adding it to the growing number of messages and reports now occupying a bag slung over his shoulder, most of them scrawled on leaves or bits of bark, Oberon smiled. "Captain, I feel compelled to inform you of how this starchy formality between us saddens me. Surely, given our history, we may address one another as equals? It seems a great pity to think that petty concerns for rank and protocol might curtail our friendship."

As per usual on those occasions when his mood was light, he addressed his old lover with a degree of flirtation, clapping a hand on his shoulder and leaning forward so that his loose silver hair brushed Bunce's cheek. Both of them knew it was sport, nothing more. As for Puck, once he had satisfied himself that Bunce was no threat, he'd encouraged Oberon to rebuild his old friendship, going so far as to suggest—albeit whilst very drunk—that the captain be invited to their bed on his birthday.

With an indulgent chuckle, Bunce replied, "Oberon, it would sadden me to watch your subjects convince themselves that you treat me with unearned favouritism. My sudden arrival and immediate promotion have already made me a few enemies."

"In truth? I was unaware," said Oberon, frowning. "Who?"

"Oh, no one important," said Bunce. "'Enemies' is overstating it, really. A remark here, a dirty look there, that's all it amounts to. No, Oberon, take that glower off your face. I don't want you charging in to fight my battles for me. That won't help at all."

"I despise gossips," Oberon muttered.

Affectionately, Bunce replied, "No, you don't. Puck's a terrible gossip, and so, for that matter, are you. My king, I tell you in all honesty, the words of jealous chatterers mean nothing to me. 'Reputation is an idle and most false imposition; oft got without merit, and lost without deserving.'"

"If memory serves, the character who spoke those lines was a villainous wretch who came to an ignoble end."

"Good William's villains tend to be his most sensible characters. They speak far more wisdom than his heroes," said Bunce. "Come. I've a few free minutes. Let's share a quick meal by the river while you look over Peaceblossom's report. She put a great deal of work into it."

"Fond of her, are you?"

Bunce coloured and mumbled something incoherent as they made their way to the river.

Soon, they both sat in the shade of an alder, watching the clouds while licking their fingers clean of the remains of a roasted sparrow. Their conversation meandered down several pleasant and trivial paths, and Oberon was admiring the first fireflies when an arrow narrowly missed his neck.

If Bunce had missed the sight of it passing, he didn't miss the sound of it hitting the alder's trunk. Immediately, he was on his feet, the shield that had been serving as a dish for his dinner held up in defense of Oberon's person.

"My liege, get down..." he began, just as two figures wearing masks and wielding daggers lunged from the shadows behind

Oberon.

Oberon's hearing was no less acute than his captain's, and he had already turned to meet them. The first assailant received a knee to the gut, followed by a slap to the face that sent him flying. The second, cleverer, came in low, and his knife would have sunk into Oberon's side had it not been for the speed of the king's reflexes. While still in the process of dispatching the first, Oberon used his free hand to take hold of the second by his wings and squeezed until he felt one crack.

As his victim screamed in pain, Oberon looked back over his shoulder to see Bunce flying off in the direction the arrow had come from, disappearing into a bush. A moment later, there was a yelp, and the bush shook. Bunce emerged dragging with him another masked assassin, whose nose was bloody and whose bowstring had been used to bind his hands behind his back.

"Sloppy work," Bunce commented, depositing the archer at Oberon's feet and kicking the other two unfortunates into line with him. "Your father attracted a far more competent breed of assassin."

"I am entirely uncertain of how to take that," said Oberon, pulling off the archer's mask. "Ah, Cobweb. How good to see you."

"Well met, my liege," Cobweb sighed with what seemed to be remarkable gentility for a fairy who had so recently attempted to take Oberon's life.

Bunce unmasked the other two. Oberon was surprised to see that the one whose wing he had broken was Redleaf, the royal treasurer. Hmm...now that he thought about it, Puck *had* said something about curtailing his expenditure, hadn't he...

"Explain yourselves!" Bunce was demanding of their captives.

Cobweb shrugged. "What is there to explain?"

"I admit, Cobweb, that I am less disappointed by your treachery than I am by your aim," said Oberon. "Why didn't you delegate the task to one of your co-conspirators? I know Redleaf is a decent shot. Or was it that you wanted the glory of being the first to draw my blood?"

"I wouldn't gloat, Oberon," spat Redleaf, and Bunce kicked him.

Cobweb didn't look irritated by the king's jibe. If anything, he looked hurt. "My liege, how could I take any pleasure in harming you? You are my cousin's husband, and our rightful king."

Baffled, Oberon said, "It's a touch late for flattery, Cobweb. You tried to put an arrow in me not two minutes ago."

"I took no pleasure in it. And I wasn't trying to kill you, I swear it. My intention was to wound."

"What rot," Bunce scoffed.

Cobweb persisted. "I can bear your wrath, my liege, but not your disdain. I beg you to understand that I am neither treacherous nor incompetent. I was not trying to usurp your throne, only to save you from yourself."

"Your words are flotsam and jetsam," said Bunce. "What could you possibly have hoped to achieve by wounding the king?"

Cobweb continued to gaze up at Oberon, his expression sad and apologetic. Then Oberon understood.

"It would prevent me from going to Puck's defense," he breathed, ice in his veins.

"I am sorry, my liege," said Cobweb. "Once that nasty little conjurer is out of the way, you will see..."

Oberon didn't hear the rest. He was already running.

Chapter Five

As he charged through the glade, knocking aside anyone and anything in his way, the king's mind churned.

Where is he?

Where had he last seen him? By the cooking fires, that was right, he'd been eating a roasted mushroom, and he'd said... What had he said? *Think*! Ah, he'd mentioned going to give the falcon its dinner. That wouldn't have taken him long, and surely, they wouldn't have attacked him out in the open?

"Puck!" he shouted, his voice carrying from one end of the glade to the other. "Where..."

He stopped, memory stirring. Hadn't Puck also said something about writing letters to the goblin tribes with whom Oberon's court had traded in the past, requesting any spare food or tools they might have to donate? He did all his formal writing in his home in the stout willow. If he'd attended to that task immediately after feeding the falcon, that was where he'd be now.

Oberon ran as fast as he could, cursing his lack of weaponry, Cobweb, the court, and every inch of distance between himself and the willow. When he got there, he scaled the trunk with reckless speed and arrived at Puck's home to find the door ajar.

There were no sounds coming from inside, and on the square foot of carpet he could see through the open door, there was a puddle of blood. For some reason, all Oberon could think was, *If he's dead, I won't be able to make him any more toast. I'll have to eat the rest of the loaf myself.*

Although songs had been sung of the fairy king's valor in battle and of his steely resolve in the face of overwhelming odds, Oberon would remain convinced for the rest of his life that pushing the door all the way open was the bravest thing he had ever done.

The blood was not a puddle, as he had first assessed, but a lake. Every inch of carpet and flooring that he could see was covered in the stuff, and there was more on the walls. Puck's acorn table had been overturned and his shelf full of enchanted oddities lay on its side, drenched in gore. Here and there, Oberon could see what looked like bits of wing.

Puck stood in the middle of the room, cleaning one of his knives. No, Oberon realized—not a knife. A pair of scissors, the same silver ones he used to trim Oberon's hair.

"Well met, master," Puck said, sounding tetchy. "Watch your step. They broke my lovely mirror and there's glass everywhere."

Although his servant was spattered with blood, what Oberon couldn't see anywhere on him were wounds of his own. Crossing the threshold, Oberon tried to count the bodies. Difficult as the task was, given that most of them were in at least two pieces, he concluded that five assassins had entered Puck's home.

"Baroness Mint is in there somewhere," Puck said. His lip curled with contempt. "She brought a sword. It wasn't even enchanted or coated with poison. Just an ordinary sword. Were your lot any better prepared?"

Oberon acknowledged his words with a slow nod, but he wasn't listening. He was having trouble concentrating on anything other than the red smudge staining his servant's delicate ankle, and another on the tip of his left wing, and another on the inside of his thigh. There was a lantern mounted on the wall behind him, giving his unruly black curls a bright halo while his face remained shadowed. The effect made his black, shining eyes all the more striking; like the eyes a hunter might see staring back at him from the depths of a cave whose entrance was littered with bones.

I want him, Oberon thought. He was surprised at himself. So great was his relief at Puck's being alive and his anger at those who had intended otherwise, he'd not have thought there was room in him for lust.

His body was insistent: *Want him. Now.*

The door was still open and a breeze was blowing in. The smell of blood was distracting. Bunce was probably waiting for him with their prisoners, or else he would have handed them over to one of his guards and come looking for him. At that moment, all those salient facts felt irrelevant.

"Oberon?" said Puck, evidently perplexed by his silence.

"Hmm?" Oberon replied, swallowing. He had vague hopes of concealing his sudden hunger. It was, after all, not the time or place. But the harder he tried to look away from Puck's body the more impossible it seemed.

Looking thoughtful, Puck finished cleaning his scissors and, putting them aside, undid the string that held up his leaf skirt. It fluttered down his long legs and landed in the blood at his feet. Holding his gaze, Puck slunk forward, placing a hand on Oberon's chest as he reached him and forcing him to stumble back until his shoulder blades hit the wall.

"Are you angry with me?" Puck asked him.

His servant's hands framed Oberon's face, flicking a lock of hair out of his eyes.

"No," Oberon told him, leaning down and pressing their foreheads together. "I am...I'm sorry I wasn't here sooner. It didn't occur to me that they'd target you too."

Puck's eyes widened in understanding. "You were afraid for me, master?"

Oberon's skin felt too tight. It was all he could do to nod.

"Tush," said Puck, tweaking his nose and unbuttoning Oberon's tunic. "However driven you are to take care of your subjects, you don't need to take care of me. I've put paid to far more interesting opponents than any of your petulant political foes."

Light as moth wings, Puck's fingers danced down Oberon's stomach, through the dense hair at his groin, and over his cock, before the sprite went to his knees.

"I note, master, that you don't appear to be sporting any injuries yourself," he said, in between dropping soft kisses against Oberon's thickening shaft. "Can I presume that their attempt on your life was equally unsuccessful?"

"Almost embarrassingly so. I swatted them aside like gnats," Oberon told him. The tips of Puck's wings were trembling, Oberon noticed, and he wondered for the first time whether he really was as unruffled by the experience as he seemed.

"I wish I could have seen that. You're magnificent when you're smiting unworthy foes."

While Puck slid his pink lips down his cock, Oberon stroked his wingtips and said, "I would hope that you'd know this without my having to say it, but just in case you don't... This ridiculous business was in no way your fault. Even if it was, I would sooner contend with a hundred assassins every morning and evening than sacrifice a minute spent in your company. I do not know what I would do without you."

Puck's mouth was too full for him to respond, but the next time Oberon ran a finger along the edge of his wing, it came away coated in golden dust. Even better, after caressing Oberon's balls Puck reached further back and pressed a finger into him, then another. Groaning, Oberon spread his legs wider, losing track of time until what little restraint he had collapsed, and he finished deep in Puck's throat.

After licking him clean, Puck said, "In answer to your question...you would shave less often, grant even more irresponsible loans to your subjects, and be more leery of having bits of metal shoved into your cock. Otherwise, I imagine you'd be fine."

"It occurs to me, impudent one, that I've not had you over my knee for some time. I shall remedy that as soon as this catastrophe has been dealt with. And you are wrong." Oberon pulled him to his feet and kissed him soundly.

Stroking Oberon's jaw, Puck replied, "No, I am not. If one day an assassin does remove me from your company, do you think you will collapse in a heap? Run wailing into the wilderness, never to be seen again? No, not my brave warrior king. You will survive. You will weep, and then you will recover and carry on. I know this. I know you."

From the open door, a voice called, "King Oberon, the captain told me to report that...oh!"

"Not now!" they snarled in one voice, and the hapless emissary fled.

☆☆☆

The trial was over and the verdict unquestioned.

"Exile?" said Puck as Cobweb and the other two surviving assassins were herded away at the point of Bunce's spear. "I'd have preferred it if you'd let me feed them to your foxes. You know they'll come back and cause trouble. Or else they'll ally themselves with Ariel."

Puck understood, though. Although they had been as discreet as possible in disposing of the corpses scattered about his home, there wasn't a fairy within a hundred miles who didn't have a rough but essentially accurate idea of what he'd done to them. It was wise of Oberon to counteract rumors of his servant's brutality with evidence of his own leniency.

"They'd make the foxes ill," said Oberon. "As for my father, he's welcome to them."

They stood together on the edge of a branch overlooking the glade, Oberon's hand resting on Puck's shoulder while Puck leaned back against his chest. In the day and a half that had passed since Mint's failed assassination attempt, Oberon had tended to clutch at whatever part of Puck happened to be within arm's reach. If any of the court objected to their king's newfound affinity for holding his servant's hand in public, the scissors which Puck now wore at his belt at all times dissuaded them from commenting.

Gazing upwards and shielding his eyes against the sunlight, Puck said, "Here she comes."

The silhouette of an eagle was visible high overhead. Puck took shelter behind Oberon's back as it dropped from the sky towards them, coming to land on the branch where they stood. It was laden with parcels, packages, and one passenger, who dismounted with feline grace while Oberon went down on one knee.

"My lady," he rumbled.

"My consort. How like a winter hath my absence been from thee," Titania replied in curt tones. "What has happened?"

"Happened? What makes you think..."

"Your servant gets a twitch when he's hiding something from me."

Oberon glared at Puck, who twitched.

"More to the point," said Titania, gazing down across the glade, "unless my memory fails me, several dozen of my most beloved trees appear to be missing."

Sighing, Oberon stood and recounted the events of the past few days with the air of a truant schoolboy called to confess his crimes to the headmaster.

"Queen Titania," Puck butted in as soon as he had finished. "You have my word that this catastrophe was beyond Oberon's power to predict and that once it unfolded he behaved with unparalleled courage and good sense. Furthermore..."

"Goodfellow, I've been traveling for half a day. My head aches, I stink of bird, and I've no desire to listen to your prattle. Make yourself useful and unload my cargo."

"You've brought home some weighty souvenirs," Oberon noted, gazing up at the eagle's burden. It was a wonder it had been able to take off at all.

"Not souvenirs. Supplies and tools. When I told her what had befallen my court, my grandmother granted me a small loan to assist in the recovery efforts, on the condition that you accompany me next time I go visit her."

Puck and his master exchanged a look. "You already knew?"

An impish smile had begun to blossom on her majesty's berry-red lips. "Of course I knew, idiot man. I knew as soon as it happened. My spies tell me everything. I also know that your servant vivisected one of my favourites, a crime for which I shall be extracting no end of favours, believe me. That said...I see the excavation is near to completion and that you've managed to maintain some semblance of order, which can't have been easy. Well done, husband. You've exceeded my expectations."

As Oberon's chest swelled like a pouter pigeon, she added, "Of course, you have left me with the unenviable task of finding a new royal treasurer, given that your profligate loans apparently drove the last one to treason."

"Lady, I think I have identified a potential candidate," said Puck. "Your handmaiden Peaceblossom—she is pragmatic and hard-working and has been invaluable these last few days. Moreover, she is a deft mathematician."

"Truly? All right, we'll give her a shot."

With palpable relief, Oberon extended his arm to the queen. "Shall we go and announce your return to your subjects?"

"Yes, let's. And afterwards, my husband, we shall discuss the matter of sound fiscal governance and policymaking..."

Puck hung back while the king and queen descended from the branch and went to greet the court. When he was sure they were both out of earshot, he looked up and said, "You can come out now, master."

Oberon jumped down from the upper branch upon which he had been lurking, concealed by the foliage.

"That went better than I'd expected," he said, as the cheers of the court reached their ears. "Even so, I'm glad we took precautions."

Puck nodded. Had Titania taken it into her head to blame her husband for the recent commotion and subject him to a tirade, Puck feared he would have lost his temper and leapt to Oberon's defense, souring his relationship with the queen. At least if she was bullying the duplicate he'd conjured up, he could simply leave and join the real Oberon in hiding until she was done.

"An unforeseen advantage is that I now have you all to myself for the rest of the day," he pointed out, sidling up to the king.

"Sprite, are you suggesting I shamelessly delegate my duties to the copy and abscond with you?"

"And with us," confirmed two more Pucks, appearing on either side of him.

☆☆☆

A short while later, Oberon had one of his Pucks nestled in his lap, his back to his chest, sighing as Oberon's cock rubbed along the cleft of his arse. The other two were caressing each other for Oberon's entertainment; he found the sight both delectable and delightfully absurd. He was feeling faintly giddy, buzzing with a mingled sense of triumph and relief now that their tribulations were, at last, at an end.

"My ears must be failing me. I could have sworn you just *giggled*," said Puck.

"Don't be ridiculous," said Oberon. He adjusted their position slightly, curling a strong arm under Puck's left thigh to spread his servant's legs further apart.

Puck shivered as Oberon's spare hand fondled his balls and said, "Wait, wait. If you want me to do this I need to concentrate."

One of the other two Pucks broke away from his partner to hand over the silver rod, cleaned and oiled.

"You don't have to if you don't…" Oberon began.

"Shush. Of course I want to. Don't worry, love, I've done it before."

As he'd promised, Puck was able to slip the rod into himself with the same grace and ease with which he could take Oberon's cock down his throat. Watching it, Oberon was dazzled by the contrast between bright silver metal and hot red flesh, and he clutched him tighter, his hips rocking forward against Puck's arse.

"S…see?" Puck gasped. "Easy. *Ah!*"

"Precious one," Oberon whispered to him, rutting against Puck's buttocks helplessly. He tried to synchronize his thrusts with the oscillating rise and plunge of the rod, and soon Puck had begun to babble expletives in his strange foreign tongue. The other two, busy fingering each other, gave identical moans, and Oberon recalled Puck's claim that they all felt one another's pleasure. It occurred to him to wonder if they might not play with *his* double, once it had departed Titania's company.

"Master," they gasped in one voice, as Oberon felt himself begin to crest.

He couldn't pinpoint the exact moment the other two Pucks disappeared. After coming, he was preoccupied with watching Puck remove the silver rod; when he looked up, they were alone.

"A successful experiment, would you say?" asked Puck, when Oberon had finished him off with his hand.

Oberon rolled the rod between his fingers, once again admiring the elegance of its construction. "Indeed. Whatever will mortals think of next?"

Both of them started as the door opened; all members of Oberon's court knew not to interrupt him when he was alone in his bedroom with Puck. But instead of a supplicant or an assassin, it was Oberon's double who entered, peering at them curiously before licking his lips.

Conscious of Puck's intent scrutiny, the reclining king beckoned the other closer. Embracing him felt strange, though not disagreeable—Oberon had never realized how large his own nose was, or how soft his lips. He kept one eye open as they kissed, watching Puck fondle himself.

"I have another experiment to propose," Oberon said when they parted.

Clapping, Puck leapt in his arms and purred as the two of them boxed him in. "Splendid, master."

About the Author

(Insert bio, 100 words max) Orci cras faucibus sociosqu adipiscing vestibulum consectetur duis risus a ac ullamcorper mi a nisl vestibulum duis praesent porta aenean curae urna felis posuere a vitae vulputate condimentum.Et gravida dolor suspendisse ac venenatis dui donec ullamcorper pulvinar cum diam erat a vestibulum magnis natoque.Sociis aliquet quisque adipiscing ridiculus curabitur lectus suspendisse orci duis fermentum enim class conubia dolor lobortis accumsan et litora suspendisse parturient dictumst laoreet dolor parturient ligula egestas.Nunc urna in vulputate adipiscing parturient adipiscing gravida egestas sed fringilla curabitur ullamcorper rhoncus eros consequat vivamus a sed accumsan nunc.Malesuada nulla parturient dapibus blandit hac dictum.

Also by T.J. Land

Adrift Series
The Captain's Men
The Captain's Encounter
The Captains' Calamity

NineStar Press, LLC

www.ninestarpress.com

www.ingramcontent.com/pod-product-compliance
Lightning Source LLC
Chambersburg PA
CBHW020338260626
47156CB00004B/1589